GOLDENBOY

By Michael Nava and also available from Alyson Books

The Little Death
How Town
The Hidden Law

GOLDENBOY

A HENRY RIOS MYSTERY

MICHAEL NAVA

alyson books
los angeles

I want to thank Kelly McCune for her advice and assistance,
Mike and Alan for their last-minute insights,
my friends on Deloz Avenue,
Bill, of course, and Sasha.

MANUFACTURED IN THE UNITED STATES OF AMERICA.

THIS TRADE PAPERBACK IS PUBLISHED BY ALYSON PUBLICATIONS,
P.O. BOX 4371, LOS ANGELES, CALIFORNIA 90078-4371.
DISTRIBUTION IN THE UNITED KINGDOM BY TURNAROUND PUBLISHER SERVICES LTD.,
UNIT 3, OLYMPIA TRADING ESTATE, COBURG ROAD, WOOD GREEN,
LONDON N22 6TZ ENGLAND.

FIRST HARDCOVER EDITION: APRIL 1988
FIRST PAPERBACK EDITION: DECEMBER 1991
SECOND EDITION: JULY 1996
THIRD EDITION: OCTOBER 2003

03 04 05 06 07 a 10 9 8 7 6 5 4 3 2 1

ISBN 1-55583-829-4
(SECOND EDITION PUBLISHED WITH ISBN 1-55583-366-7.)

LIBRARY OF CONGRESS CATALOGING-IN-PUBLICATION DATA
    NAVA, MICHAEL.
        GOLDENBOY : A HENRY RIOS MYSTERY / MICHAEL NAVA.
        I. TITLE.
    PS3564.A8746G64
    813'.54—DC20   96-21334 CIP

CREDITS
COVER PHOTOGRAPHY BY DERIN THORPE.
COVER DESIGN BY MATT SAMS.

Ah, Spencer
Since words are crude and only stand between
Heart and heart, and understanding fails us
There's nothing left amid such deafness but bodily
Contact between men. And even that is very
Little. All is vanity.

The Life of Edward the Second of England
— Bertolt Brecht

— 1 —

"You have a call."

I looked up from the police report I had been reading and spoke into the phone intercom. "Who?"

"Mr. Ross from Los Angeles."

"Put him through." I picked up the phone thinking it had been at least a year since I'd last talked to Larry Ross.

"Henry?" It was less a question than a demand.

"Hello, Larry. This is a surprise."

"Are you free to come down here and handle a case?"

I leaned back into my chair and smiled. Born and bred in Vermont, Larry retained a New England asperity even after twenty years in Beverly Hills where he practiced entertainment law. His looks fit his manner: he was tall and thin and beneath the pink, nude dome of his head he had the face of a crafty infant.

Rejecting a sarcastic response — Larry was impervious to sarcasm — I said, "Why don't you tell me about it."

"It's the Jim Pears case. Have the papers up there carried anything about it?"

I thought back for a minute. "That's the teenager who killed one of his classmates."

"Allegedly killed," Larry replied, punctiliously.

"Whatever," I said. "I forget the details."

"Jim Pears was working as a busboy in a restaurant called the Yellowtail. One of the other busboys named Brian Fox caught Jim having sex with a man. Brian threatened to tell Jim's parents. A couple of weeks later they found the boys in the cellar of the restaurant. Brian had been stabbed to death and Jim had the knife."

"Airtight," I commented.

"No one actually saw Jim do it," he insisted.

I turned in my chair until I faced the window. The rain fell on the green hills that rose behind the red-tiled roofs of Linden University. That last weekend of September, winter was arriving early in the San Francisco Bay.

"That's his defense — that no one actually saw him do it? Come on, Larry."

"Hey," he snapped, "whatever happened to the presumption of innocence?"

"Okay, okay. Let's presume him innocent. What stage is he at?"

"The Public Defender has been handling the case. Jim pled not guilty. There was a prelim. He was held to answer."

"On what charge?"

"First-degree murder."

"Is the D.A. seeking the death penalty?"

"No," Larry replied, uncertainly, "I don't think so. But isn't that automatic if you're charged with first-degree murder?"

"No." I reflected that, after all, criminal law was not Larry's field. "The D.A. has to allege and prove that there were special circumstances surrounding the murder which warrant the death penalty."

"Like what?" Larry asked, interested.

"There are a lot of them, all listed in the Penal Code. Lying in wait, for instance. There's also one called exceptional depravity."

"Not just your garden-variety depravity," Larry commented acidly. "Only a lawyer could have written that phrase."

"Well, figuring out what it means keeps a lot of us in business," I replied, glancing at my calendar. "When does Pears's trial begin?"

"Monday."

"As in two days from today?"

"That's right," he said.

"I'm missing something here," I said. "The trial begins in

two days and tne ooy is represented by the P.D. Am I with you so far?"

"Yes, but — " he began, defensively.

"We'll get to the buts in a minute. Isn't it a little late to be calling me?"

"The P.D.'s office wants to withdraw."

"That's interesting. Why?"

"Some kind of conflict. I don't know the details."

Almost automatically I began to take notes, writing 'People v. Pears' across the top of a sheet of paper. Then I wrote 'conflict.' To Larry I said, "You seem to know a lot for someone who isn't involved in the case."

"Isn't the reason for my interest obvious?"

I penned a question mark. "No," I said, "better explain."

"Everyone's abandoned him, Henry. His parents and now his lawyer. Someone has to step in — "

"I agree it's a sad situation. But why me, Larry? I can name half a dozen excellent criminal defense lawyers down there."

"Any of them gay?"

"Aren't we beyond that?"

"You can't expect a straight lawyer to understand the pressures of being in the closet that would drive someone to kill," he said.

I put my pen down. "What makes you think *I* understand?" I replied. "We've all been in the closet at one time or another. Not many of us commit murders on our way out."

There was silent disappointment at his end of the line and a little guilt at mine.

"Look," I said, relenting, "how does Jim feel about me taking the case?"

"I haven't spoken to him."

"Recently?"

"Ever."

"Customarily," I said, "it's the client who hires the lawyer."

"His P.D. says he'll go along with it."

"Go along with it? I think I'll pass."

"Jim needs you, Henry," Larry insisted.

"Sounds to me that what he needs is a decent defense. I'm not about to take a case two days before it's supposed to go to trial even if Jim himself asked me. I'm busy enough up here."

"Henry," Larry said softly, "you owe me."

In the silence that followed I calculated my debt. "That's true," I replied.

"And I'm desperate," he continued. Something in Larry's voice troubled me — not for Jim Pears, but for Larry Ross.

"Are you telling me everything?" I asked after a moment.

"I need to see you, Henry," he said. "I'll fly up tonight and we'll have dinner. All right? I'll be there on the five-fifteen PSA flight."

"That'll be fine, Larry." I said goodbye.

After I hung up, I went across the hall to Catherine McKinley's office. She and I had both worked as public defenders and had remained friends after leaving the P.D. Now and then we referred clients to each other, though this happened less often as she took fewer and fewer criminal defense matters, preferring the greener pastures of civil law. I had remained in the trenches.

Her secretary, a thin young man named Derek, was taping a child's drawing to the side of his file cabinet. The drawing depicted a green house with a lot of blue windows, a red roof, a yellow door and what appeared to be an elephant in the foreground.

"Is your daughter the artist?" I asked.

He turned to me and smiled. "It's our house," he replied.

"And your pet elephant?"

"That's the dog. You want to see her?" he asked, gesturing toward Catherine's closed door.

"If she's not busy."

He glanced at the phone console. "Go ahead," he said, and handed me a bulky file. "Would you give this to her?"

"Sure."

I knocked at the door. Catherine said, "Come in."

In contrast to my own office which could charitably be described as furnished, Catherine's office was decorated. The color green predominated. Dark green wallpaper. Wing chairs uphol-

stered in the same shade. All the green, she told me, was to provide subliminal encouragement to her clients to pay their bills.
It must have worked because she looked sleeker by the day.

She glanced up at me with dark, ironic eyes. Catherine was
a small, fine-boned woman, not quite pretty but beside whom
merely pretty women looked overblown. I set the file at the edge
of her desk.

"What's this?" she asked, laying an immaculately mani-
cured finger on the folder.

"Derek asked me to bring it in."

She smiled. "I didn't think he was your type."

"I was on my way in anyway," I said, dropping into one of
her money-colored chairs. "I may need a favor."

She raised a pencilled eyebrow.

As I told her about Larry's call the eyebrow fell and the
shallow lines across her forehead deepened. When I finished she
said, "You can't really be thinking about taking the case."

"I'm afraid I really am," I replied. "Larry wouldn't have
called me if it wasn't important, much less remind me that I
owe him..." I let the sentence trail off.

Catherine filled in the blank. "Your life?"

I shrugged. "My professional life, anyway."

"Still," she said dismissively. "Sounds like a slow plea to
me."

"Maybe."

"What's the favor?"

"If I take the case I'll need someone to stand in for me on my
cases up here. Just to get continuances."

"It'll cost you, Henry," she warned.

I smiled. "My professional life?"

"We'll start with lunch," she replied. "Get me a list of your
cases and we'll discuss them then. Is that it?"

I stood up. "For now. Thanks, Cathy."

She looked at me. "Don't you ever get tired of losing,
Henry?"

I thought about this for a second. "No," I said.

□

It was still raining when I left my office at six to meet Larry's plane at the San Francisco airport. The wind was up, scattering red and yellow leaves like bright coins into the wet, shiny streets. A stalwart jogger, wrapped in sweats, crossed the street at the light and I felt a twinge of regret. The only kind of running I did these days was between courts. Still, a glance in the mirror reported no significant change in my appearance from my last birthday — my thirty-sixth. The light flashed green and I jostled my Accord forward onto the freeway ramp.

I entered a freeway that was clogged with Friday night traffic. Sitting there, watching the rain come down, gave me time to think. It wasn't true that I never got tired of losing. Only three years earlier I had been tired enough of it to resign from the P.D.'s office, expecting to abandon law altogether. But I had fallen in love with a man who was murdered. Hugh Paris's death led me back into law though I took a lot of detours getting there. One of them was through the drunk ward of a local hospital. I might have been there yet had it not been for Larry Ross and the United States Supreme Court.

The summer I entered the drunk ward was the same summer that the Supreme Court, in a case involving Georgia, upheld the right of states to make sodomy — a generic term for every sexual practice but the missionary position — illegal. Within weeks there was a move to reinstate California's sodomy law, which had been repealed ten years earlier, by a special election. A statewide committee of lawyers was organized to fight the effort. Larry Ross, a hitherto closeted partner in a well-known Los Angeles firm, chaired the committee. He needed a lawyer from northern California to lead the effort up here. After asking around, he found me, or rather, what was left of me.

We went into the campaign with the polls running against us. Larry poured all his energy and a quarter of his net worth — which was considerable — into trying to change the numbers. Halfway through, however, it was plain that we would lose. Since we couldn't win the election, we decided to try to knock the sodomy initiative off the ballot with a lawsuit. We went directly to the state Supreme Court, arguing that the initiative violated the right to privacy guaranteed by the state constitution.

Two days before the ballot went to the print shop, the court ruled in our favor. It looked like a victory but it wasn't. We had merely prevented things from getting worse, not improved them. Since then, some part of me had been waiting for the next fight. Maybe Larry had found it in this Pears case.

I pulled into a parking space at the airport and hurried across the street to the terminal. I was nearly twenty minutes late. Coming to the gate I saw Larry in a blue suit, raincoat draped over one arm and a briefcase under the other. He was far away yet I could hardly fail to recognize his spindly stride and the gleaming dome of his head.

Then, coming closer, I thought I had made a mistake. The man who now approached me was a stranger. The flesh of his face was too tight and vaguely green in the bright fluorescent light. But it was Larry. The edges of his mouth turned upward in a smile.

"Henry," he said embracing me, or rather, pulling me to his chest, which was as far up on him as I came.

I broke the embrace and made myself smile. "Larry."

He looked at me and the smile faded. I looked away.

It was then I noticed the odor coming off his clothes. It was the smell of death.

— 2 —

To cover my shock at his appearance I asked, "Do you have any luggage?"

"No, I'm catching the red-eye back to L.A. Where are we eating?"

I named a restaurant in the Castro. As we talked, he looked less strange to me, and I thought perhaps it was only exhaustion I saw on his face. He worked achingly long hours in the bizarre vineyard of Hollywood. We talked of small things as I drove into San Francisco. We came over a hill and then, abruptly, the city's towers rose before us through the mist and rain, glittering stalagmites in the cave of night, and beyond them, sensed rather than seen, the wintry tumble of the ocean.

We rolled through the city on glassy streets shimmering with reflected lights. On Castro, the sidewalks were jammed with men who, in their flak jackets, flannel shirts, tight jeans, wool caps and long scarves, resembled a retreating army. I parked and we walked back down to Nineteenth Street to the restaurant. Inside it was dim and loud. Elegant waiters in threadbare tuxedos raced through the small dining rooms with imperturbable poise. We were seated at a table in the smaller of the two dining rooms in the back with a view of the derelict patio just outside. Menus were placed before us.

"It's really good to see you," Larry said, and picked up his menu as if not expecting a response. I ventured one anyway.

"You've been working too hard," I said.

"I suspect you're right," he replied.

I dithered with the menu as I tried to decide whether to pursue the subject.

"What you want to say," Larry said, "is that I look terrible."

"You look—" I fumbled for a word.

"Different?" he asked, almost mockingly. He lit a cigarette and blew smoke out of the corner of his mouth away from me. I waited for him to continue. Instead, the waiter came and Larry ordered his dinner. When it was my turn I asked for the same.

We sat in nervous silence until our salads were brought to us. The waiter drizzled dressing over the salads. Larry caught my eye and held it. When the waiter departed, Larry picked up his fork, set it down again and relit his discarded cigarette.

"I'm dying, Henry," he said softly.

"Larry—"

"I was diagnosed eight months ago. I've already survived one bout of pneumocystis." He smiled a little. "Two years ago I wouldn't have been able to pronounce that word. AIDS has taught me a new vocabulary." He put out his cigarette.

"I'm so sorry," I said stupidly.

The waiter came by. "Is everything all right?"

"Yes, fine," Larry said.

"Why didn't you tell me sooner?" I asked.

"There was nothing you could have done then," he said, cutting up a slice of tomato.

"Is there now?"

"Yes. Defend Jim Pears." He put a forkful of salad in his mouth and chewed gingerly.

"I don't understand."

"I'm going to die, Henry," he said slowly. "Not just because of AIDS but also because the lives of queers are expendable. Highly expendable." He stopped abruptly and stared down at his plate, then continued, more emphatically. "They hate us, Henry, and they'd just as soon we all died. I'm dying. Save Jim Pears's life for me."

"Don't die," I said, and the words sounded childlike even to my own ears.

"I won't just yet," he replied. "But when I do I want it to be my life for Jim's. That would balance the accounts."

"But it's entirely different," I said.

"It's the same disease," he insisted. "Bigotry. It doesn't matter whether it shows itself in letting people die of AIDS or making it so difficult for them to come out that it's easier to murder."

"Then you do think he did it."

"Yes," he said. "Not that it makes any difference to me."

"It will to a jury."

"You'll have to persuade them," he said, "that Jim was justified."

"Self-defense?"

Larry said, "There might be a problem there. Jim's P.D. told me Jim doesn't remember anything about what happened."

"Doesn't remember?" I echoed.

"She called it retrograde amnesia."

The waiter came and took Larry's salad plate. He cast a baleful glance at my plate from which I had eaten nothing and said, "Sir, shall I leave your salad?"

"Yes, please."

We were served dinner. Looking at Larry I reflected how quickly we had retreated into talk of Jim Pears's case as if the subject of Larry's illness had never been raised.

"I want to talk some more about you," I said.

Larry compressed his lips into a frown. "I've told you all there is to know."

"How do you feel about it?"

"Henry, I've turned myself inside out examining my feelings. It was painful enough the first time without repeating the exercise for you."

"Sorry." I addressed myself to the food on my plate, some sort of chicken glistening with gravy. A wave of nausea rose from my stomach to my throat.

Larry was saying, "But I won't go quietly. Depend on that."

We got through dinner. Afterwards, we went upstairs to the bar. Sitting at the window seat with glasses of mineral water we watched men passing on the street below us in front of what had been the Jaguar Bookstore.

Abruptly, Larry said, "I wondered at first how I could have been infected. It really puzzled me because I thought AIDS was only transmitted during tawdry little episodes in the back rooms of places like that." He gestured toward the Jaguar. "All my tawdry little episodes were twenty years in the past, and then there was Ned." Ned was his lover who had died four years ago.

"Were you monogamous with Ned?"

He smiled grimly. "I was monogamous, yes."

"But not Ned."

"You don't get this from doorknobs, Henry." He frowned.

"Do you think he knew?"

"He killed himself didn't he?" Larry snapped. "At least now I know why," he added, quietly.

"Who have you told?"

"You."

"That's all?"

He nodded. "My clients are movie stars. Having a gay lawyer is considered amusing in that set but a leper is a different matter."

"But — your appearance."

"You haven't seen me in, what? A year? And even you were willing to accept the way I look as the result of overwork. It's not really noticeable from day to day."

"But you must have been in the hospital?"

"With the flu," he said. "A virulent, obscure Asian flu with complications brought on by fatigue."

"People believed that?"

"People are remarkably incurious and besides. . ." He didn't finish his sentence. He didn't have to. I knew he was going to say that people preferred not to think about AIDS, much less believe that someone they knew had it. I was struggling with my own disbelief and, at some deeper level, my terror.

"How long can you keep it a secret?"

"Henry, you're talking to a man who was in the closet for almost thirty-five years. I know from secrets." He yawned. "I'd like to go for a walk down by the water, then we have to talk some more about Jim Pears."

It had stopped raining by the time we reached Fisherman's

Wharf but that loud, normally crowded, arcade of tourist traps and overpriced fish restaurants was deserted anyway. We walked around aimlessly, jostling against each other on the narrow walks, stopping to comment on some particularly egregious monstrosity in the shopfront windows. We walked to the edge of the pier where the fishing boats were berthed, creaking in the water like old beds. A rift in the clouds above the Golden Gate revealed a black sky and three faint stars. Larry looked at them and then at me.

"Do you wish on stars, Henry?" he asked.

"Not since I was a kid."

"I do," Larry replied. "Wish on stars. Pray. Plead. It doesn't do any good." We stood there for a few more minutes until he complained of the cold.

I drove us to Washington Square and we found an espresso bar. Tony Bennett played on the jukebox. We each ordered a caffe latte. Larry brought out a bulky folder from his briefcase and put it on the table between us.

"What is it?" I asked.

"My file on Jim Pears. You're taking the case, aren't you?"

I hesitated. "Yes. I'll fly down on Monday morning. Will I have a chance to talk to Jim before the hearing?"

"I don't know. You'll have to ask his P.D. A woman named Sharon Hart." He paused and sipped his coffee. "She's not a bad lawyer but something's not working out between her and Jim."

"It happens. I'm always running up against the expectations of my clients. You learn to be tactful."

Larry wasn't listening. He was looking at his reflection in the window. When he looked back at me, he asked, "Do I seem hysterical to you?"

I shook my head.

"I do to myself sometimes." He rattled his cup. "I'm so angry, Henry. When I wake up in the morning I think I'll explode from rage."

He tightened his jaw and clamped a hand over his mouth.

"Don't you expect that?" I asked, awkwardly.

He lowered his hand, revealing a faintly hostile smile. "You've been reading too much Kubler-Ross," he said. "There are only two stages to dying, Henry. Being alive and being dead. We treat death like a bad smell. I'm supposed to excuse myself and leave the room."

His eyes were bright. It was the only time I had ever seen Larry even approach tears and it was frightening.

"Why should you care what other people think? You never have before."

"Well, that's not true," he snapped. "I was the original closet queen, remember?" He expelled a noisy breath, then sipped from his coffee. "I don't know why I'm taking it out on you."

"Because I'm here?"

He shook his head. "Because I love you." He tried to smile but his face wouldn't cooperate. "I'll miss you."

He lowered his face toward the table and I watched the tears slide down his cheeks and splatter on the table top. I reached for his hand and held it. After a moment or two it was over. He looked up, drew a dazzlingly white handkerchief from his breast pocket and wiped his face.

He glanced at his watch. "It's the witching hour. You'd better get me back to the airport."

I pulled up in front of the terminal and helped Larry gather his things. He put his hand on the door handle.

"Wait," I said.

He looked over at me. I leaned across the seat and kissed him.

"I love you, too," I said.

"I know."

A moment later he was gone.

— 3 —

It was nearly one when I pulled into the carport and parked in my allotted space. It was raining again and a heavy wind rattled the treetops filling my quiet street with creaks and wheezes. I grabbed the bulky folder Larry had given me and made a run for my apartment, stopping only to collect my mail and a soggy edition of the evening paper.

Inside I was greeted by silence. The only unusual thing about this was that I noticed it at all. I put the folder on my desk, added the paper to the stack in the kitchen and leafed through the bills and solicitations that comprised my mail. I turned on a burner and poured water into the tea kettle, set it on the flame, opened a bag of Chips Ahoy and ate a few. When the water was boiling I poured it into a blue mug with "Henry" emblazoned on it — the gift of a client — and added a bag of Earl Grey tea. Then there was that silence again. It seemed to flow out of the electrical outlets and drip from the tap.

Only the silence was not quite silent enough. It was filled with my loneliness. I had lived alone long enough and I did not want to die this way. These days, death no longer seemed like such a distant prospect to me. I sipped my tea. I thought of my empty bed. I opened the folder and found the transcripts of Jim Pears's preliminary hearing.

□

The purpose of a preliminary hearing is to see whether the prosecutor can establish probable cause to bring the defendant to trial — to "hold him to answer," in the arcane language of the law. For the defense, however, the prelim is an opportunity to preview the prosecution's evidence so as to prepare to refute it at trial. Consequently, the prosecutor puts on as little evidence as possible to show probable cause, holding what he can in reserve.

The transcripts of Jim's prelim consisted of two slender volumes. The events leading up to Brian Fox's death were narrated by two witnesses who had also worked at the restaurant. The first was a waiter named Josh Mandel. I set my cup down and began reading:

Frank Pisano, D.A.: At some point prior to Brian Fox's death, did you have a conversation with Brian about Jim Pears?

Mrs. Sharon Hart, P.D.: Objection, calls for hearsay.

Pisano: This statement is admissible under section 1350 of the Evidence Code. We filed some papers —

The Court: I have them here.

Pisano: Yes, Your Honor. Uh, we expect Mr. Mandel will testify that he was told by Brian Fox that he — Brian — saw Jim Pears engaging in sex with a man. That's relevant to the issues here and Brian Fox is certainly unavailable, thanks to Mr. Pears.

The Court: Mrs. Hart?

Hart: There're a lot of conditions here that have to be satisfied before 1350 applies. Like — for example, the statement has to have been written down or tape-recorded.

The Court: Where is that? Oh, all right, I see it. What about that, Mr. Pisano?

Pisano: It also says it's okay if the statement is made under circumstances that indicate its trustworthiness. That's an alternative to a taped or written statement.

Hart: No it's not. That's in addition to.

The Court: Well, I tend to agree with the prosecutor on that. I'm going to let the statement in.

Hart: Defense objects.

The Court: Understood. The objection's overruled.

Pisano: Do you remember the question, Josh?

Josh Mandel: Yeah. Brian told me he had proof that Jim was gay.

Pisano: Do you mean homosexual?

Hart: Objection, leading.

The Court. We're wasting time. Overruled. Answer.

Mandel: Yes.

Pisano: Did he tell you what this proof was?

Mandel: Yes.

Pisano: What was it?

Mandel: He said he saw Jim having sex with some guy in a car out in the restaurant parking lot.

Pisano: How long before Brian was killed did you have this conversation with him?

Mandel: A couple of weeks.

Pisano: Now, did you ever overhear a conversation between Brian and Jim Pears regarding this incident in the parking lot?

Mandel: Well, I think. Yeah. They were talking about it.

Pisano: What was said?

Hart: Objection, hearsay.

Pisano: This is an admission, Your Honor.

The Court: Let's hear it. Answer the question, Mr. Mandel.

Mandel: Brian was asking Jim how would he like his mother to know that he was— (Inaudible.)

Pisano: You'll have to speak up, Josh.

Mandel: A cocksucker. I'm sorry, Your Honor, but that's what he said.

The Court: I've heard worse things in this court, Mr. Mandel. Next question, counsel.

Pisano: Okay. Did Jim Pears say anything in response?

Mandel: Yeah.

Pisano: What?

Mandel: He said something like, 'I'll kill you before that happens.'

Pisano: And how soon before Brian's murder did this conversation take place?

Mandel: It was two days.

(Cross-examination by Mrs. Hart)

Hart: Now you say that Brian Fox told you he saw Jim having sex with a man that night, is that right?

Mandel: Yes.

Hart: This was in a private car in the parking lot at night?

Mandel: Yeah, I guess.

Hart: Did Brian explain how he happened to be there?

Mandel: Not to me.

Hart: Well, isn't it true that Brian Fox followed Jim and then snuck up on him?

Pisano: The People will stipulate that Brian was not asked to join in on the festivities.

The Court: Why don't we let the witness answer, Mr. Pisano?

Mandel: I don't know.

Hart: Now, Mr. Mandel, what words did Brian use to describe what he had seen?

Mandel: I don't remember, exactly.

Hart: Well, did he say he'd seen Jim having sex or making love?

Mandel: No. It was more like he saw him getting a blow job.

Hart: Okay. Did you ever hear Brian Fox call Jim a faggot?

Pisano: Objection, irrelevant.

The Court: Overruled. Answer the question.

Mandel: Yes.

Hart: More than once?

Mandel: Yes.

Hart: Did you ever hear Brian Fox call Jim a queer?

Mandel: Yes.

Hart: More than once?

Mandel: Yes.

Hart: How many times did you hear Brian Fox call Jim either a faggot or a queer?

Mandel: I don't remember.

Hart: Isn't it true that you don't remember because that was how Brian normally referred to Jim?

Mandel: He called him that a lot.

Hart: Around other people?

Mandel: Yes.

Hart: Now, Mr. Mandel, isn't it true that, in addition to being a waiter at the Yellowtail, you are also a manager?

Mandel: Manager-trainee.

Hart: And isn't part of your job to supervise the busboys on the shifts that you manage?

Mandel: Yes.

Hart: And did you ever manage a shift where Brian and Jim were working?

Mandel: Yeah.

Hart: And during one of those shifts did you hear Brian call Jim a queer or a faggot?

Mandel: I'm not sure. Maybe.

Hart: But you never stopped Brian, did you?

Mandel: I don't remember.

Hart: In fact, isn't it true that you also called Jim a faggot once?

Mandel: I don't remember.

Hart: Isn't it true that you told Jim to start acting like a man?

Mandel: That was just because he was letting Brian get to him.

Hart: Then shouldn't you have talked to Brian?

Mandel: Yeah. (Inaudible) I'm sorry, Jim.

Hart: I have nothing further, Your Honor.

(Examination by Mr. Pisano of Andrea Lew, a cocktail waitress at the Yellowtail.)

Pisano: Who was working at the Yellowtail between eleven-thirty p.m. and midnight on the night Brian was killed?

Lew: It was just me and Frank — that's the bartender — and Jim was the busboy.

Pisano: Besides the bar was any other part of the restaurant open?

Lew: No, the kitchen closes at ten.

Pisano: How many people were in the bar at that time?

Lew: Not many. It was Monday, you know. Slow night. Maybe a dozen.

Pisano: Between eleven-thirty and midnight did you see anyone enter the bar?

Lew: Just Brian.

Pisano: Now, would you have noticed if anyone else had come in?

Lew: Well, yeah, because you have to cross in front of the bar to get to the dining rooms or the kitchen.

Pisano: Was Jim Pears in the bar when Brian came in?

Lew: Yes.

Pisano: Did he see Brian?

Mrs. Hart: Objection, calls for speculation.

The Court: Sustained.

Pisano: Okay. Was Brian working that night?

Lew: No, just Jim.

Pisano: Do you know what he was doing there?

Lew: (Shakes head.)

Pisano: You're going to have to answer yes or no for the reporter.

Lew: No.

Pisano: Did you see Brian leave the bar at some point?

Lew: No, but he was gone.

Pisano: Did you see Jim Pears leave the bar?

Lew: Yes.

Pisano: When was this?

Lew: Maybe around midnight.

Pisano: Where did he go?

Lew: Back toward the kitchen.

Pisano: Did you also go back to the kitchen at some point?

Lew: Yes.

Pisano: Why?

Lew: There's a movie theater next door and around midnight the last show gets out. Some people came in for a drink and Frank needed some more ice so he told me to have Jim bring him up some.

Pisano: Where is the ice kept?

Lew: In the walk-in — that's the refrigerator — in the kitchen.

Pisano: About what time was it when you went back into the kitchen?

Lew: A quarter after twelve.

Pisano: Did you see Jim back there?

Lew: No.

Pisano: What did you do?

Lew: It's hard ... I ...

Pisano: One step at a time, Ms. Lew, and we'll get through this. He wasn't in the kitchen. Then what?

Lew: I looked in the locker room. I looked outside, out the back door, but he wasn't there.

Pisano: Was the back door unlocked?

Lew: Yeah.

Pisano: Okay. He wasn't in the kitchen, the locker room, or outside. Then what did you do?

Lew: I looked in the walk-in. He wasn't there. That left, the only place was the cellar. That's where I went.

Pisano: I want you to describe the cellar, Ms. Lew.

Lew: There's a big room where the wine's kept. Then there's two little rooms, one for the manager's office. The other one is where we keep the hard liquor.

Pisano: Did you go into the cellar?

Lew: Yes.

Pisano: What did you find in the big room?

Lew: Nothing. I called Jim but he wasn't there.

Pisano: What did you do then?

Lew: It was kinda creepy down there. I was going to get Frank's ice myself but then—

Pisano: We're almost done, Ms. Lew.

Lew: I'm sorry. The manager's office was closed up. I saw that the door to the liquor room was open a little and the light was on. I went over and then — there was this noise, like a whimper. Like a puppy makes. I thought maybe Jim was lifting boxes and hurt himself so I went in.

Pisano: What did you see?

Lew: The first thing was just Jim. He was kinda hunched over and leaning against some boxes. There was a funny smell, like a bottle of liquor got broken so I looked down at the floor. That's when I — saw him.

Pisano: Saw who, Ms. Lew?

Lew: Oh, God, I didn't know at first. His face was all — but then it was the clothes Brian was wearing in the bar. There was blood. I looked back at Jim. He was holding one of the kitchen knives and his hands were bloody. There was blood on his shirt and his pants like he tried to wipe the knife clean.

Pisano: Did he speak to you?

Lew: No. I don't know. I ran out of there and started screaming for Frank as soon as I was upstairs.

Pisano: Then what happened?

Lew: Frank came to the back and there was some other guys with him, from the bar, I guess. I told them what was downstairs. We piled things up against the cellar door and called the police.

Pisano: And when did they arrive?

Lew: Five, ten minutes. It seemed like forever before I heard the sirens.

Pisano: That's all, Ms. Lew. Thank you.

The Court: Cross-examination, Mrs. Hart.

Hart: I have no questions of this witness.

▫

The bloody images of Brian Fox's murder remained with me even after I set the transcripts aside and made myself another cup of tea. Coming back to my desk, I picked a looseleaf binder out of the folder Larry had given me and opened it up. Inside were press accounts of the Pears case from the day Jim was arrested to the day after he'd been held to answer. I flipped the pages until I came to a story that had a picture.

The headline proclaimed "The Tragic Death of Brian Fox." Beneath the headline was a black-and-white of Brian that startled me for no better reason than his youth. I had cast someone older and sleazier for the role of the boy who tormented Jim Pears. Instead, I found myself looking at a handsome boy with light hair whose features had not yet set on his slightly fleshy face. His half-smile revealed either shyness or surprise. There was a caption beneath the picture: "His mother called him golden boy."

I read the story. It consisted of lachrymose interviews with Brian's mother, teachers, and fellow students. You'd have thought he was in line for sainthood, at least. I looked back at the face. No hint of sainthood there. Maybe the twist of the smile was neither shyness nor surprise. Maybe it was sadism. I wondered, would a jury buy that? Probably not.

I went back and read the stories in chronological order. Jim had not fared nearly as well as Brian. The only picture of him showed him lifting his handcuffed wrists to his face as he was led into court for arraignment. The first spate of stories were more or less straightforward accounts of what had occurred at the Yellowtail that night. They tallied with the cocktail waitress's testimony.

Subsequent stories, ignoring the possibility of Jim's innocence, dwelt on his motive for killing Brian. Much was written about what were termed Brian's "teasing" remarks about Jim's homosexuality. There were inaccurate reports of the parking lot incident. According to one paper, it was Brian himself to whom Jim offered sex. Another paper got most of the details right but the reporter termed Brian's activities a "prank." The upshot was that Jim was a psycho closet case with a short fuse that Brian accidentally ignited.

The last batch of stories was the worst. Oddly enough — or perhaps not — Jim's father, Walter Pears, was responsible for these stories. Jim's parents had resisted the media until just before the prelim. Then his father had talked. Walter Pears's explanation for Jim's crime was "demonic possession." He announced that since Jim was apparently in the thrall of Satan, the best that could be done was, as the elder Pears said repeatedly, to "put him away for everyone's good."

The press took up the notion of satanism. There were rumors about the alleged disfigurement of Brian Fox's body. A priest made the connection between homosexuality — an abomination before God — and worship of the devil by whom, presumably, such practices were tolerated. At length, the coverage grew so outrageous that the chief of police himself felt constrained to deny that any evidence of devil-worship or demonic possession existed in the case.

I reached the end of the binder. A first-year law student could predict the result of this case. Jim's trial would merely be a way station on the road to prison. Keeping him off death row would be as much victory as anyone could reasonably expect. It was nearly three in the morning. I finished my tea and got ready for bed.

— 4 —

The storm that passed through San Francisco on Friday had worked its way through Los Angeles by the time I stepped off the plane on Monday. It was a distinctly tropical eighty degrees that last morning of September. I threw my overcoat into the back of my rented car and made my way downtown to the Criminal Courts Building.

The vast city was just awakening as I sped eastward on the Santa Monica Freeway. I had spent a lot of time in Los Angeles when I worked with Larry on the sodomy lawsuit two years earlier. I knew the city as well as anyone who didn't live there could, and I liked the place. Between the freeway and the Hollywood Hills the feathery light of early morning poured into the basin and it truly did seem, at that moment, to be the habitation of angels. The great palms lifted their shaggy heads like a race of ancient, benevolent animals. Along the broad boulevards that ran from downtown to the sea, skyscrapers rose abruptly as if by geologic accident but were dwarfed by the sheer enormity of the plain.

I parked in the lot behind the Criminal Courts Building across from City Hall and walked around to the courthouse entrance on Temple. In the space between the entrance platform and the ground lay the charred remains of a campfire, with people sleeping in rags and old blankets. Inside, the walls of the foyer were covered with gang graffiti. After an interminable wait, an elevator picked me up and ascended, creaking its way to the floor where the Public Defender had his offices. I walked into a small reception room, announced myself to the receptionist and sat down to wait. The room was crowded with restless children and adults sitting nervously on plastic chairs. A little boy came up and stared at me with wide, black eyes.

"Are you my mama's P.D.?" he asked.

I smiled at him. "No."

"Then how come you wear a suit?"

A stout woman called from across the room, "Leave the man alone, Willie."

"I'm waiting for my P.D., Willie," I said.

"Nah," he replied, and went back to his mother.

The door beside the receptionist's desk opened. A short, heavy gray-haired woman in a bright floral dress said, "Henry Rios."

I stood up.

"I'm Sharon Hart," she said. "You want to come into my office?"

I followed her through the door and we picked our way down a hallway lined with metal file cabinets into a small office. There was a calendar on one wall and framed degrees on the other. Sharon Hart sat down behind her government-issue desk and motioned me to sit on one of the two chairs in front of it. She pulled an ashtray out of her desk and lit a cigarette.

"So," she said. "You're the famous Henry Rios."

There was nothing particularly hostile in her tone so I ventured a smile.

"I hope you can walk on water, Mr. Rios, because that's the kind of skill you're going to need on this case."

"Is that why you're getting out?"

She looked at me sharply. "I'm not afraid of tough cases."

"Then why withdraw?"

"This case is indefensible on a straight not-guilty plea."

"There are alternatives."

She shook her head. "Not with this client. He won't agree to any defense that admits he did it."

"Any chance he didn't do it?"

Her look answered my question.

"Then that could be a problem," I said.

"He's also going to make a lousy witness," she said offhandedly. "Not that there's much for him to say. He doesn't remember what happened."

"So I was told. Retrograde amnesia, is that it?"

She nodded. "I had the court appoint a shrink to talk to him. You'll find his name in the files." She gestured to two bulky folders lying at a corner of her desk. "The doctor says it's legitimate. Jim doesn't remember anything between opening the cellar door and when that girl — the waitress — came down and found him with Brian Fox."

"Is he crazy?"

She smiled slightly, showing a crooked tooth. "My shrink will say that he was at the time of the murder."

"Not quite the question I asked," I murmured.

"Is he crazy now? Let's say the pressure's getting to him."

"Where's he being held?"

"County jail," she said.

"You've told him what's going to happen this morning?"

"Yes," she said. "He'll agree to it." She stubbed out her cigarette and lit another. "We don't get along," she added. "Call it ineffective empathy of counsel. But I do feel sorry for the kid. I really do." She stood up. "Take the files. You'll find my investigator's card in them. He can fill you in. We better get downstairs. Pat Ryan runs a tight ship."

"The judge."

"Patricia Ryan."

"Irish."

Sharon smiled. "Black Irish, you might say."

Television cameras were set up in the jury box and the gallery was packed with reporters. To avoid the press, we had come in through the corridor that ran behind the courtrooms. As soon as we reached counsel's table, though, the cameras started rolling. At the other end of the table a short, dark-haired man was unpacking his briefcase.

"The D.A.," Sharon whispered. "Pisano."

"What's he like?" I asked.

She shrugged. "He's decent enough until you get him in front of the cameras."

"A headline grabber?" I asked.

"The worst."

As if he'd heard, the D.A. smiled at us, then turned his attention to a sheaf of papers that he was marking with a red pen.

"Where's Jim?" I asked.

"In the holding cell, I guess," she said. "They won't bring him out until she takes the bench."

I looked over my shoulder at the reporters. "This is quite a circus," I said.

"Better get used to it."

A middle-aged woman with stiffly coiffed hair and dressed in black stared at Sharon Hart and me with intense hostility from the gallery.

"Who's that?" I asked.

Sharon glanced over. "Brian Fox's mother. She comes to every hearing. You'll like her."

"What about Jim's parents?"

"Oh, them," she said venomously. "They're just as nice as Mrs. Fox."

In a seat across the aisle from Brian's mother sat a young man in a blue suit, wearing horn-rimmed glasses. My eye caught his for a moment, then he looked away.

"That's Josh Mandel," Sharon said.

"Oh," I replied, glancing at him once again.

She looked at me. "Do you know him?"

"No," I said, and yet he seemed somehow familiar.

The bailiff broke the silence of the courtroom with his announcement. "Please rise. Department Nine is now in session, the Honorable Patricia Ryan presiding."

The judge came out from behind the clerk's desk through the same door by which we had entered. Patricia Ryan was a tall black woman whose handsome face was set in a faintly amused expression.

In a pleasant, light voice she said, "Good morning, counsel. Please be seated." She looked down at her desk. "People versus Pears. Is the defendant in court?"

A blond court reporter clicked away at her machine taking down every word.

"He's coming," the bailiff said.

The door to the holding cell opened and the TV cameras swung away from the judge over to the two marshals who escorted Jim Pears into the courtroom. I had just enough time to glance at him before the judge started talking again. They sat Jim down beside Sharon Hart at the end of the table.

"We were to begin the trial of this matter today," the judge said. "However, ten days ago the Public Defender's office filed a motion to withdraw from the case. Is that correct Mrs. Hart?"

"Yes."

The judge looked at me quizzically and said, "Who are you, sir?"

"Henry Rios, Your Honor. I've been asked to substitute in should the Public Defender's motion be granted."

"Thank you, Mr. Rios. All right. The defendant is now present and represented. The People are represented and are opposing this motion."

"That's right, Your Honor," Pisano said.

"Mrs. Hart, you go first."

Sharon Hart stood up. "The People complain about delay," she began, "without showing that their case would be prejudiced by the delay. They don't say either that witnesses or evidence would become unavailable to them if the trial is postponed. My client, on the other hand, has a constitutional right to effective representation. My office can't provide that at this point. So it seems to me, Your Honor, that if you weigh his rights against the prosecution's pro forma objection, it's clear the motion should be granted."

The judge said, "Mr. Pisano."

"Your Honor," he said. "the D.A.'s office is not a lynch mob. We want Mr. Pears to get a fair trial. Our objection is that the P.D.'s office has completely failed to tell anyone why it can't handle this case. Now," he said, stepping back from the table and coming up behind Sharon Hart, "we saw how well Mrs. Hart conducted the defense during the prelim—"

"Thanks," Sharon whispered mockingly.

"—so what's the problem now? They say they have a conflict. What conflict?" He shrugged eloquently. "Surely we all want to see that justice is done as expeditiously as possible."

"I'm sure," Judge Ryan replied with a faint smile. She was clearly aware that Pisano was playing to the press.

Undeterred, he continued. "We don't know what the conflict is and I would hate to suspect that this motion is only to delay things, but. . . ." He left the end of the sentence dangling, with another shrug of his shoulders. "And what about our friend, Mr. Rios," Pisano continued. "He's not going to be ready to start trying the case today. No, he'll be asking for time. Maybe a lot of time. Maybe, considering the People's evidence, forever."

Sharon Hart seethed. I composed my face into the mask I reserved for such occasions.

"Or maybe," Pisano said, "there's another reason for this motion. Mr. Rios here is not unknown. He was one of the lawyers who knocked the sodomy initiative off the ballot a couple of years ago. He represents a powerful constituency."

"I hardly see—" the judge began.

"Your Honor, if I may finish," Pisano cut in, his voice darkening theatrically. "Let me suggest that this motion is the result of political pressure on the P.D.'s office by the gay community to let Mr. Rios try the case. . . ." Again Pisano let the end of his sentence trail off suggestively.

I heard the rustling of papers in the gallery as the reporters scribbled their notes. Pisano would make the news tonight.

"I really must object," Sharon Hart said. "That remark is completely improper."

The judge glowered at the D.A. "Mr. Pisano, that comment is not well taken."

"My apologies," the D.A. said smoothly. "Perhaps I spoke out of turn. But the court must understand the People's frustration. This motion is so mysterious, Your Honor. I'm completely at a loss as to why a perfectly competent lawyer like Mrs. Hart wants off this case."

"Mrs. Hart."

"Your Honor, it took me a minute but I finally understand what the D.A. is up to. He wants me to put on the record why my office can't represent Mr. Pears. We obviously can't do that without compromising the defense. This court will simply have to accept my representation that an irreconcilable conflict exists between me and Mr. Pears."

The judge's eyebrows darted up. Judges do not appreciate being told what they must accept.

"Nonetheless," the judge observed, "the motion is discretionary with me."

Seeing her mistake, Sharon said, "I didn't mean to suggest otherwise, Judge. I'm just saying the prosecution wants a sneak preview of the defense. They're not entitled to that."

Pisano broke in. "Your Honor, as you point out, granting or denying this motion is your choice. I just don't see how you can make a fair decision based on some vague representation of irreconcilable conflicts. We're not talking no-fault divorce here."

"Anything else?" Judge Ryan asked, looking at Hart and Pisano.

"Submitted," both lawyers said in unison.

The judge stared uneasily into space.

"What's she thinking?" I whispered.

"She's thinking that if she grants the motion she'd better have a good reason because the D.A. will file a writ petition in the Court of Appeal before the ink is dry on her order," Sharon whispered back.

I heard the clink of metal and remembered that Jim Pears, who had been ignored during the hearing, was still sitting at the end of the table.

"What does Jim—" I began.

"Shush," Sharon snapped. The judge had begun to speak.

". . . concerned, Mrs. Hart, that I don't have enough of a basis to rule intelligently on your motion. Now I can appreciate you not wanting to tip your hand to the prosecution. So what I think I'll do is take Mr. Rios, you and the reporter into chambers and have you put the conflict on the record. I will then order that portion of the transcript sealed. Is that acceptable?"

I watched the struggle in Sharon's face. She clearly thought her word that a conflict existed should be enough, but she also wanted to win.

"Yes, Judge," she said.

"What about the People?" the D.A. asked.

"What about the People?" the judge repeated with exasperation.

"Well, I thought—"

"Nice try, Mr. Pisano," the judge said. "Court's in recess. Mrs. Hart, Mr. Rios."

We followed her back across a corridor into her chambers and sat down while she took off her robe and hung it up. There was a framed law degree on the wall from Stanford and, next to it, a picture of the judge shaking hands with the Democratic governor who had appointed her to the bench. The windows of her office overlooked City Hall and the Times-Mirror Building. She sat down behind a vast rosewood desk.

"All right," she began briskly. "We're in chambers on People versus Pears. Mrs. Hart, tell me about this conflict." The reporter's fingers flew across the keyboard of her machine as the judge spoke.

"My client refuses to cooperate in preparing a defense," she said.

"He wants to plead guilty?" the judge asked.

"No, he insists he's not guilty."

Judge Ryan grinned. "Most defendants do, Mrs. Hart."

"That's not a tenable defense," Sharon insisted.

The judge nodded, thoughtfully. "Unless you have a secret weapon, the evidence presented at the prelim seems pretty conclusive."

"There is no secret weapon," Sharon said. "At least in regards to whether he did it. But, as to why he did it..." She let the sentence trail off.

"I understand," the judge said.

We were at a delicate point. Since Judge Ryan would be presiding at the trial there was a limit to what Sharon Hart could disclose to her about the defense without laying the judge open to a charge of being less than completely impartial.

"Anyway," Sharon continued, "I feel very strongly that I cannot continue to represent Mr. Pears and I think he feels just as strongly that he can't work with me, either."

The judge turned to me. "Mr. Rios."

"I'm willing to try the case on terms set by my client."

The judge arched an eyebrow. "Have *you* read the transcript of the preliminary hearing?"

"Yes. However, Judge, whatever the state of the evidence, there comes a point when you have to do what your client wants — if, in good conscience, you can."

The judge frowned but said nothing.

"He's right, Judge," Sharon said, coming to my rescue. "It's Jim who's on trial here."

The judge looked at the reporter and said, "This is off the record." The reporter stopped typing and the judge said, "Do you really think Jim Pears has the wherewithal to call the shots in this case?"

Sharon and I exchanged surprised looks.

"Now I know I'm speaking out of turn," the judge continued, "but when I look at Jim Pears all I see is fear. I'm going to grant your motion, Sharon, and I'll give you some time to prepare for trial, Mr. Rios, but I want you to know that I feel very strongly that this is not a case that should be coming to trial. There should be a disposition."

"The D.A.'s not giving an inch from murder one," Sharon said sourly.

Judge Ryan set her mouth into a grim smile. "The D.A.," she said, "can be persuaded. All right. You think about what I've said, Mr. Rios. Now let's go out and do this on the record."

"Yes, Judge," we both chimed.

We preceded her into the court. I asked Sharon what that was all about.

"It sounds to me like she doesn't want a jury to get their hands on Jim. If I were you, I'd consider waiving a jury and having a court trial."

I stopped at the table where Jim was sitting and leaned over. "Jim, my name is Henry," I whispered.

He looked up at me and said, "I didn't do it."

— 5 —

Sharon Hart's motion was granted and I was substituted in as Jim Pears's attorney of record. The trial date was continued to December first to give me time to prepare. After the ruling was made the D.A. stood up.

"Yes, Mr. Pisano," the judge said.

"The People wish to move to amend the complaint."

The judge looked annoyed. "This isn't exactly timely notice, counsel."

"The Penal Code says the People can move to amend at any time," Pisano replied blandly.

"There's a difference between what's permissible and what's fair," she snapped. "What's your amendment?"

Sharon Hart moved to the edge of her seat. Pisano took out a stack of papers and passed a set of them to me. The other set he handed to the bailiff who took them to the judge. I glanced at the caption. It was a motion to amend the complaint and allege special circumstances to the murder charge.

"You're seeking the death penalty?" the judge asked. Behind us, the gallery murmured. The bailiff called the courtroom into order.

"Yes, Your Honor," Pisano replied.

Sharon Hart said, audibly, "Bastard."

"At the preliminary hearing you said this wasn't a special circumstances case," Judge Ryan said.

Contritely, Pisano replied, "I was wrong. We have reviewed the transcripts of the prelim and looked at our evidence. We now think we can show special circumstances."

I got to my feet. "Your Honor, I'm not prepared to respond to this motion at this time. I'd ask that it be put over for a couple of weeks to give me time to file an opposition."

"Fine," she said. "File your papers within twenty-one days. I will hear arguments a month from today. Court is adjourned."

The judge left the bench and the bailiff cleared the courtroom of reporters. The deputies who had been standing beside Jim got him to his feet.

"When can I talk to my client?" I asked one of them.

"He'll be back at county this afternoon."

"Jim, I'll be there later."

He stared past me and nodded. They led him off.

The courtroom cleared out quickly, until only Sharon Hart and I were left.

"You coming?" I asked her.

"Not through that door," she said, indicating the front entrance. I remembered the reporters and the TV cameras. "You?" she asked.

"If I don't," I said, "Pisano will have the boy convicted and sentenced by the six o'clock news."

"See you," she said, and slipped out the back.

□

"Mr. Rios, can you answer a few questions?" I stood in a semicircle of reporters, the TV cameras running behind us in the busy corridor outside the courtroom. Pisano — to his chagrin, I imagined — commanded a smaller group down the hall.

"Sure," I said. I heard the clicking of cameras as a couple of photographers circled.

"What do you think about the D.A. seeking the death penalty?"

"It's an obvious attempt to extort a guilty plea from my client," I replied.

"Why did the Public Defender withdraw from the case?"

"Irreconcilable conflicts," I said.

"What were they?"

"That's information protected by the attorney-client privilege," I replied.

"What's your defense going to be?"

"Not guilty."

"What about the evidence?"

"What about it?"

"It's pretty strong."

"Strong is not good enough," I said. "It has to be," and I repeated the ancient charge to the jury, "beyond a reasonable doubt and to a moral certainty. I expect to show that it's not."

"How?"

Good question, I thought. To my interrogator, though, I said, "I'm not free to disclose the details of our investigation."

"What about the political pressure by gays that the D.A. talked about? Is that true?"

"As counsel for the People conceded, he was speaking out of turn."

"Then it's not true?"

"Of course not."

"But you are gay aren't you?"

I turned to face the person who had asked the question. It was Brian Fox's mother. She was trembling with anger.

"Yes, I am, Mrs. Fox, for what that's worth."

"You're all thick as thieves," she said while the cameras turned on her. "All of you — faggots. What about my boy? He's dead."

"Yes, I know," I said, and stopped myself from expressing condolences. It would only give her another opportunity to attack. "I expect the facts surrounding his death will come out at trial. All of them, Mrs. Fox."

We glared at each other. Her face was rigid. She pulled her head back, drew in her cheeks and spat, hitting my neck. The TV cameras recorded the incident. I wiped my neck with my handkerchief. She turned away and clicked down the hall.

"There's your lead," I told the reporters.

□

From the courthouse I drove to Larry Ross's house. Though he worked in Beverly Hills he lived in Silver Lake, a hilltop community east of Hollywood and far from the currents of fashion on the west side of the city. Silver Lake was a reservoir named in honor of a turn-of-the-century water commissioner, but the fortuitous name aptly described the metallic sheen of the water which was not quite a color but a quality of light.

There were hills on both the east and west sides of the lake. Larry lived in the west hills on a street where the architecture ran the gamut from English Tudor to Japanese ecclesiastical Stucco was the great equalizer. Larry's house was sort of generic Mediterranean. From the street it appeared as a two-storey white wall with an overhanging tile roof, small square windows on the upper floor and a big, dark door set into an arched doorway on the lower. I parked in the driveway and let myself in.

From the small entrance hall, stairs led up to the guest rooms on the second floor. The kitchen was off to the right. To the left there was an immense boxy room that terminated in a glass wall overlooking a garden composed of three descending terraces and the reservoir at the bottom of the hill. The room was furnished with austere New England antiques but its austerity was lightened by elegant pieces of Chinese pottery, Oriental carpets, and wall-hangings like the parlor of a nineteenth-century Boston sea captain made prosperous by the China trade. It was a room designed for entertaining but its stillness indicated that it had not been used for that purpose for a long time, since Ned's suicide.

After Ned's death, Larry had built another wing onto the house, where he now lived. It consisted of a loft bedroom that looked out over his study and the garden.

I went upstairs where I would be staying while I was in town. In a study on the second floor I read rapidly through the files that Sharon Hart had given me. I noted the name of her investigator, Freeman Vidor. I also found the name of the psychiatrist, Sidney Townsend, who had examined Jim. There was no report from the psychiatrist. I called him, reaching him just as he was about to begin a session. He told me to come by in an hour. Freeman Vidor was out, but I left a message on his machine. Finally, I called Catherine McKinley, who had spent the morning in court attempting to continue my cases and then in my office fending off clients.

"What happened in court?" I asked her.

"I got three continuances and disposed of two other cases.

That frees you up for at least a couple of weeks. How are you?"

"Trial's set in six weeks. My client wants a straight not guilty defense."

"On the facts you told me?"

"That's right."

"The kid has a death wish."

"Then he may get it," I replied. "The D.A. wants to amend and add special circumstances."

"That just occurred to him?" she asked, incredulously.

"He's playing to the press," I replied. "I don't know how serious he actually is about amending."

"Any chance the kid's not guilty?"

"I asked the very same question of the P.D. who was handling the case. She rolled her eyes."

"That must mean no," Catherine said. "What are you going to do, Henry?"

"Larry Ross sees Jim as a victim of bigotry against gays," I said. "That's what he wants to put on trial."

"I don't see how that changes the evidence."

"Agreed. But it might change the way the jury looks at the evidence."

"I don't know, Henry," she said. "I think people are tired of being told they have to take the rap when someone else breaks the law."

"Larry's point is that in this society it's easier to kill than to come out. That's not so far-fetched."

"Not if you're gay," she replied. "Most people aren't."

"Would you buy it, Catherine?"

"Yes," she said after a moment's pause. "And I'd still vote to convict."

"You're a hard-hearted woman," I joked.

"That's right," she said seriously. "And I'm not even a bigot."

We said our goodbyes and I sat at the desk in the study looking out the window to the lake below.

□

Sidney Townsend looked exactly like what I imagined someone named Sidney Townsend would look like. He concealed the shapelessness of his body in an expensive suit but his face was big, florid, and jowly. His hair was swept back against his head and held fixedly in place by hairspray. Small, incurious eyes assessed me as he smiled and shook my hand.

He led me into his office, a tastefully furnished room that was nearly as dark as a confessional. Perhaps he specialized in lapsed Catholics, I thought, or maybe the dimness was evocative of a bedroom in keeping with psychiatry's obsession with sex. I sat down on a leather sofa while he got Jim's file. He joined me, sitting a little too close and facing toward me, his jacket unbuttoned and his arm draped across the back of the sofa, leaning toward me. The perfect picture of candor. I drew back into my corner.

"So," he said, "you're taking Jim's case to trial."

"So it appears. Do you get many appointments from the court?"

"It's probably a quarter of my practice," he said. "Does that bother you?"

"I just like to know," I said. "I wouldn't want the D.A. to be able to call you a professional witness."

"I have a whole response worked out for that," he said with a confident smile.

I bet you do, I thought. Aloud I said, "I'd like to know something about Jim Pears."

"Oh," Townsend said, offhandedly, "a typical self-hating homosexual."

"Typical?"

He shrugged. "I know that the A.P.A. doesn't consider homosexuality to be a mental disease," he said, "but let's face it, Mr. Rios, many if not most homosexuals have terrible problems of self-esteem. I see a lot of instability among them."

"You think being gay is a mental disorder per se?" I asked, keeping my voice neutral.

"That's not what I said," he replied tightly, then added, "You're gay yourself, aren't you?"

"Is that relevant?"

He smiled and shrugged. "To whether you retain me, probably." He studied me. "I'm not the enemy, Mr. Rios."

I looked back at him warily. "Okay, you're not the enemy. Why don't we talk about Jim."

He picked up a folder and opened it. "Jim says he's known about his homosexuality from the time he reached puberty," Townsend said. "He's had sexual relations with men for the last couple of years. Typical bathroom pickups, parks, that sort of thing. The incident in the restaurant was consistent with his pattern of sexual behavior."

"Which incident?"

"The man he was discovered with," Townsend said, "was a customer in the restaurant who picked him up and took him out to his car for sex. That's where this other boy — Fox? — found them."

"These sexual encounters sound risky," I said.

"They are. Maximally so, but then, Jim wanted to get caught."

"Is that what he says?"

"No, but it's obvious, isn't it?"

"What seems obvious to me," I said, "is that the reason a gay teenage boy has sex in public places is because he has nowhere else to go."

Townsend looked as if the thought had not occurred to him. "Possibly," he said.

"I was told that Jim doesn't remember anything about the actual killing," I said.

"That's right," Townsend replied. "It's a kind of amnesia induced by the trauma of the incident. It's fairly common among people who were in serious accidents."

"Not physiological at all?"

"He was given a medical examination," Townsend said. "Nothing wrong there. It's psychological."

"Aren't there ways to unlock his memory?" I asked.

"As a matter of fact," Townsend said, "I tried hypnosis."

"Did it work?"

"No. People have different susceptibilities," he explained. He thought a bit. "There are drugs, of course. Truth serums. I doubt they would work, though. He's really built a wall up there."

"Are you treating him at all?"

"That's not really my function, is it? My examination was entirely for forensic purposes."

"What about his parents? Have you talked to them?"

"They wouldn't talk to me. They're strict Catholics who don't trust psychiatry."

"They'd rather believe their son is possessed by the devil," I observed, bitterly.

"Which is simply an unschooled way of describing schizoid behavior," Townsend explained.

"Who's schizoid?"

"Jim, of course. He's completely disassociated himself from his homosexuality."

"Can you blame him?"

"I've given you my views on homosexuality," Townsend replied tartly.

"No doubt you shared them with Jim as well."

His small eyes narrowed. "I said I wasn't the enemy."

"Because you're not actually malicious?"

"Do you want me to testify or not?" he snapped.

"No, I don't think so."

He looked at me, then shrugged. "I still have to bill you for this time."

"Sure." I got up to leave.

"Mr. Rios," he said, as I reached the door. "You're making a mistake, you know. I'm the best there is."

"So," I said, "am I."

— 6 —

The sheriffs brought Jim into the conference room and seated him across from me at a table divided by a low partition. The walls were painted a grimy pastel blue that made the room look like a soiled Easter egg. The lights were turned up to interrogation intensity and I got my first good look at Jim Pears.

His fingernails were bitten down to ragged stubs. His face was white to the point of transparency and a blue vein pounded at his temple as if trying to tear through the skin. Splotches of yellow stubble spotted his chin and cheek. His hair, unwashed and bad-smelling, was matted to his head. The whites of his eyes were streaked with red but the irises were vivid blue — the only part of his face that showed life.

His eyes were judging me. It was as if I was the last of a long line of grown-ups who would fail him. It annoyed me. His glance slipped away.

"I'm sorry I wasn't able to talk to you this morning," I said. "Do you understand what happened in court?"

In a soft voice he answered, "You're my lawyer now."

"That's right. We have to be ready to go to trial in six weeks."

He shrugged and stared at the partition between us. After a moment his silence became hostile.

"Is anything wrong, Jim?"

"I don't like lawyers," he announced.

"You've got lots of company."

His face remained expressionless. "She didn't believe me," he said. "Do you?"

"That you didn't kill Brian Fox?"

He nodded.

I make it a point not to lie to my clients, but this can involve something short of the truth. I said, "I'm willing to start from that assumption."

His face was suspicious. "What do you mean?"

"What matters is convincing a jury that you're innocent," I explained.

Now he understood. "You don't believe me, either."

"I have an open mind," I replied.

He withdrew again into a sulky silence. I decided to wait him out and we sat there as the minutes passed.

"I can't sleep at night," he said abruptly.

"Why?" I wondered if he was going to confess.

"They leave the lights on. It hurts my eyes."

"It's just so the guards can keep an eye on things."

"Nothing happens in there." He looked at me. "I'm with the queens. That's what they call them."

"You're safer there than in the general population."

"They're like women," he continued, ignoring me. "They say things that make me sick." He shuddered. "I'm not like that."

"Not like what, Jim?"

"Gay." He spat out the word. Once again, his eyes drifted away. He seemed unable to look directly at anything for longer than a few seconds.

"Whether you're gay doesn't make any difference in jail," I said. "There are guys here who would claw through the walls to get at you."

His face shut down. "You're gay," he said.

"That's right."

"Gay lawyer," he said, mockingly. "Do you wear a dress to court?"

The taunt was so crude that at first I thought I'd misheard him. It was something that a six-year-old might say.

"I don't give a damn whether you think you're gay or not, Jim. That's the least of your worries."

"I'm sorry," he mumbled. "You made me mad," he added. "I didn't kill Brian."

"Then who did?" I demanded.

His shoulders stiffened. "Someone else."

"Someone else is not going to be on trial. You are. And you are also the only witness to what happened in the cellar. So unless you cooperate with me, I'd say your chances of getting out of here are pretty damn slim."

"I don't remember," he whined.

"Then you might as well fire me and plead guilty," I replied.

His face began to disintegrate into a series of jerks and twitches. At that moment, his father's theory of demonic possession seemed almost plausible.

"My head hurts," he whimpered. "I want to go back to my cell."

"All right. We're not getting off to a very good start but I'll be back tomorrow. I'll be back every day until you remember what happened that night."

"I'll try," he said.

I sat in my car in the parking lot beneath the jail surprised at the violence of my dislike of Jim Pears. I didn't usually speak to a client the way I had spoken to Jim. Part of my anger was a response to his childish insult which would have been comical except for what it revealed about the state of his self-awareness. He told me he wasn't gay with the desperation of someone who could not allow himself to believe anything else. His panic had calcified and become brittle. He was on the verge of shattering. But instead of sympathy for him I felt impatience. With his life at stake there was no time to waste while he sorted himself out.

Then I thought of how he had been unable to even look at me, and my impatience thawed a little. He had been alone in the dark for a long time and now, abruptly, he'd been yanked into the light. All he wanted was to cover his face as if he could make the harsh world disappear simply by closing his eyes to it. Perhaps he could be reached by a simplicity equal to his own. But simplicity was not among my bag of tricks.

□

Larry's Jaguar was already in the garage when I pulled in. I found him in the kitchen watching a portable TV as he chopped boiled potatoes into cubes.

"You're a star," he said.

I watched myself on the TV. A reporter explained that Jim's trial had been continued because he changed lawyers. Larry washed lettuce in the sink, drowning out the set. I turned it up.

" . . . accused of the brutal slaying of Brian Fox. Today, prosecutors moved to seek the death penalty."

Larry shut off the water. "The death penalty?"

"Wait. I want to hear this."

"The D.A. also questioned the motives behind the change of attorneys. Pears's new lawyer is Henry Rios, a prominent Bay Area attorney who is also openly gay. The D.A. suggested that pressure from the gay community to have a gay lawyer try the case led to today's hearing."

"Asshole," Larry said.

"Meanwhile," the reporter continued, "there was a dramatic confrontation outside the courtroom between Rios and the victim's mother, Lillian Fox."

We watched Mrs. Fox spit at me. I shut the television off.

"You've had quite a day," Larry said, arranging lettuce leaves in a big wooden bowl.

"I'm thinking that it was a mistake for me to have taken the case," I said.

He opened a can of tuna fish, drained and chopped it and added it to the salad. "Because the D.A. called you a carpetbagger?"

"No," I said. "It's the client. I talked to him this afternoon."

"And?" He quartered tomatoes, sliced green beans.

"He says he's not gay."

Larry looked over at me. "The kid killed someone rather than come out of the closet. What did you expect him to say?"

"He also says he didn't do it. That's why the P.D. got out of the case. He won't plead to anything."

Larry added the finishing touches to the salad and put a couple of rolls into the microwave.

"You of all people should know that there are ways of bringing clients around," Larry said.

"I don't like him."

"Oh." He wiped his hands on a towel and poured himself a

glass of water. "Why?"

"He makes me feel like a faggot," I replied.

"Well," Larry smiled. "Aren't you?"

"Come on, Larry. You know what I mean. His self-loathing is catching."

"Let's eat," Larry said. "Then we'll talk."

After dinner we sat on the patio. The wind moved through the branches of the eucalyptus trees that lined the lake. A yellow moon rose in the sky. A string of Japanese lanterns cast their light from behind us. Larry lit a cigarette.

"Those can't be good for you, now," I said.

"They never were," he replied. "Did I tell you about the cocktail party tomorrow?"

"If you did I don't remember."

"It's a fundraiser for Jim's defense."

"I suppose I have to go," I said, unhappily.

"I'm afraid so," he replied. He shrugged. "These people want to help Jim."

"He's not much interested in helping himself."

"What's bothering you about this case?"

"I told you."

"You don't have to like him."

"He tells me he didn't do it," I said. "Which means he's either not guilty or he can't bring himself to admit his guilt. The first possibility is remote."

"Maybe he thinks he was justified," Larry offered.

I shook my head. "No, I believe he thinks he didn't do it. This amnesia—"

"That's deliberate?"

"It certainly allows him to deny knowledge of the only evidence that could resolve this case one way or the other."

The smoke from Larry's cigarette climbed into the air. A faint wind carried the scent of eucalyptus to us from the lake.

"What bothers me," I said, "is that he insists he's innocent when he so clearly isn't."

"It must be a pretty horrible thing to admit you killed someone," Larry said quietly.

"Not someone like Fox," I said, "who made Jim suffer and who he must hate."

"Then maybe it was death," Larry said. "Being in that room with a man he had killed. Once you've seen death unleashed, it pursues you." He sat forward, his face a mask in the flickering light of the lanterns. "Maybe that's what he's running from, Henry."

□

The next morning I went to see Freeman Vidor, who had been investigating Jim's case for the Public Defender. His office was in an old brownstone on Grand Avenue which, amid L.A.'s construction frenzy, seemed like a survivor from antiquity. The foyer had a marble floor and the elevator was run by a uniformed operator who might have been a bit player when Valentino was making movies.

Freeman Vidor was a thin black man. He sat at a big, shabby desk strewn with papers and styrofoam hamburger boxes. A couple of framed certificates on the walls attested to the legitimacy of his operation. I also noticed a framed photograph — the only one on the wall — that showed a younger Vidor with two other men, all wearing the uniforms of the L.A.P.D. He now wore a wrinkled gold suit and a heavy Rolex. He had very short, gray hair. His face was unlined, though youth was the last thing it conveyed. Rather, it was the face of a man for whom there were no surprises left. I doubted, in fact, whether Freeman Vidor had ever been young.

We got past introductions. He lifted the Times at the edge of his desk and said, "I see you made the front page of the Metro section."

"I haven't read the article," I replied and glanced at it. There was my picture beneath a headline that read: "S.F. Lawyer to Defend Accused Teen Killer."

"Teen killer," I read aloud.

"Sort of jumps out on you, doesn't it?" he replied. "Listen, you want some coffee? I got a thermos here."

"No, thanks."

He poured coffee into a dirty mug, added a packet of Sweet

'n Low and stirred it with a pencil.

"I read the report you prepared for Sharon Hart," I said.

"That's one tough woman," he replied.

"She jumped at the chance to dump Jim's case."

"I said tough, not stupid." He sipped the coffee and grimaced.

"Is there an insult in there for me?"

He smiled. "Only if you're in the market for one. All I meant is, that boy's only hope is to get a jury to feel sorry for him because this Fox kid was harassing him about being a homosexual." He finished the coffee. "But first you got to convince them it ain't a sin to be gay."

"This is Los Angeles, not Pocatello."

He lit a cigarette. "Yeah, last election a million people in this state voted to lock you guys up."

"That was AIDS."

"You tell someone you're gay," he replied, "and the first thing they do after they shake your hand is get a blood test."

"Including you?"

"It's not on the list of my biases," he said. "You want to tell me about yours?"

"Some of my favorite clients are black."

He thought about this, then laughed. "You want me in the case?"

I nodded.

"A hundred-and-fifty a day plus expenses."

"That's acceptable."

He blew a stream of smoke toward a wan-looking fern on a pedestal near the window. "Who's paying?"

"There are some people who would like to see Jim Pears get off on this one."

He smiled. "Your kind of people?"

"That's right."

"If my mama only knew." He opened a notebook and extracted a black Cross pen from the inner pocket of his jacket. "What do you want me to do?"

"I want background on Brian Fox."

He raised a thin eyebrow. "Background?"

"Whatever you can find that I can use to smear him," I explained.

He nodded knowingly. "Oh, background. What else?"

"I read in the prelim transcript that there's a back entrance to the restaurant."

"The delivery door. It was locked."

"Lock implies key, or keys. Find out who had them and what they were doing that night."

"You're fishing," he said.

"I want to know."

He made a note and shrugged. "It's your dime."

— 7 —

The cocktail party for Jim's defense fund was being held in Bel Air. I heard Larry pull into the driveway at a quarter of six, straightened the knot in my tie, put on my jacket and went downstairs to meet him. He was just entering the house as I came down.

He looked up at me and smiled. "You sure you don't mind this?"

"What, the party?"

He nodded and tossed a bundle of mail on a coffee table. He looked tired.

"Are you feeling okay?" I asked as he dropped into a chair.

"No, not really," he replied. He rubbed his temples and shut his eyes. His breath was shallow and strained. I switched on a lamp and sat down on the sofa across from him.

"I could go alone," I said.

Without opening his eyes, he smiled. "It's asking a bit much for the lamb to lead itself to slaughter," he replied.

"It can't be that bad. Who's going to be there?"

He opened his eyes. "Just the L.A. chapter of HomIntern."

"HomIntern?"

"Homosexual International," he replied and yawned. "I told a few of my friends about Jim's case and a couple of them volunteered to kick in money to help pay the legal costs. One thing led to another and the next I knew Elliot Fein was calling and offering his house for a fundraiser."

"Elliot Fein, the ex-judge?" I asked, impressed. Fein was a retired court of appeals judge and a member of a wealthy family whose patriarch had made his money in movies.

"The same," Larry said, kicking off his huge penny-loafers. He put his long, narrow feet on the table. "I could hardly refuse. Really all they want to do is get a look at you," he added. "See what they're getting for their money."

"You think they'll be satisfied?"

He gave me the once-over. "I guarantee it. How was your day?"

I told him about my meeting with Freeman Vidor. "You know what's beginning to bother me?" I said. "The fact that everybody — including his ex-lawyer, his shrink, and now Vidor — is so quick to write Jim's chances off."

Larry's smile was fat with satisfaction. "I knew I'd hired the right man for this job."

"Well," I said defensively, "the presumption of innocence has to mean something."

The smile faded. "Oh, he's an innocent, all right," Larry said, and drew out a cigarette from his pocket.

"I wish you wouldn't smoke so much."

"Please." He lit the cigarette with his gold lighter.

"Obviously he killed Brian," I said, picking up the thread of my earlier thought, "but killing is not necessarily murder."

Larry put his shoes on. "And that's what you're here to prove. We better get going."

"You're sure you want to go?"

"I'll be fine."

The sun had already set but, as we headed west on Sunset, there was still a dreamy light at the edge of the horizon and above it the first faint stars. We passed UCLA. Larry signaled a turn and we entered the west gate of Bel Air, up Bellagio. We passed tall white walls as we ascended the narrow, twisting road. From my window I watched the widening landscape of the city below and the breathless glitter of its lights. As with most cities, Los Angeles was at its most elegant when seen from the aeries of the rich.

At the top of the hill, Larry began a left turn past immense wrought iron gates opened to reveal a driveway paved with cobblestones. A moment later a house came into view. It seemed to consist of a single towering box though, as we slowed, I could see there were two small wings, one on either side. A boy in black slacks, a white shirt and a lavender tie directed us to stop. Another boy, similarly dressed, opened my door.

"Good evening, sir, how are you?" he asked as I stepped out of the Jaguar.

"Fine, thanks, and you?"

"Oh, fine, sir." He seemed startled that I'd bothered to reply.

Larry came around to me and said, "Ready, counsel?"

"Let's go."

The first thing I noticed when we stepped into the house was the size of the room we had entered. Its walls were roughly the dimensions of football fields and to say that the space they enclosed was vast exhausted the possibilities of the word. The second thing I noticed was that the far wall, except for a fireplace that could easily have accommodated the burghers of Calais, was glass. The city trembled below.

"Where do the airplanes land?" I whispered to Larry as we entered the room. Little clumps of people, mostly men, were scattered amid the white furnishings.

"None of that," he replied. "Here comes our host."

I expected the owner of the house to be dwarfed by it, but Elliot Fein didn't even put up a fight. He was a shade over five feet and his most distinctive feature was his glasses. They were perfectly round and bright red. His skin was the color of dark wood, his hair was glossy black and his face was conspicuously unlined. I guessed, from his effort to conceal it, he must be nearing seventy.

"Larry," he said in a wheezy voice. They exchanged polite kisses.

"This is Henry Rios," Larry said.

"Why haven't I met you before?" Fein asked by way of greeting.

I couldn't think of any reason except the absence of twenty or thirty million dollars on my part. This didn't seem to be the tactful answer so I said, "I don't know, but it's a pleasure, Justice Fein."

He took my extended hand and held it. "Elliot to my friends. We're all so glad you agreed to take the boy's case."

"Thank you." I attempted to regain possession of my hand but he wasn't through with it yet.

"You know," he said confidentially, "I sat in the criminal division of superior court for years before I was elevated. From what I know about Jim Pears's case, it's going to be rough sledding."

"An unusual metaphor for Los Angeles," I observed.

He looked puzzled, then dropped my hand. "Comments like that go right over a jury's head," he said with a faked smile.

I made a noise that could be interpreted as assent.

"Who's the judge?" he asked.

"Patricia Ryan."

"Good. Very good," he replied judiciously. "I'll call her for lunch next week." He beamed at us. "I'm neglecting my duties. Let me get you a drink."

"Thanks, but I don't drink," I said.

His eyes narrowed and he nodded. "Oh, that's right. Perrier, then?"

"Nothing, thank you," I replied. I felt a flash of irritation at Larry who had obviously told Fein I was an alcoholic.

"What about you, Larry?" Fein asked.

"Not just yet. I think I should take Henry around."

"Of course," Fein said, and stepped aside. "I'll talk to you later."

We started across the hall and Larry said, in a low voice, "I know what you're thinking but I didn't tell him."

"Then how did he know?"

"He's like God, only richer. So I'd watch the wisecracks if I were you."

For the next hour we worked the room. The crowd consisted of well-dressed, expensively scented men and a few women all of whom, like Fein, had found ways to slow time's passage. Larry and I fell into a routine. He would introduce me. Someone would inevitably ask what I thought of Jim's chances. I would launch into a lengthy explanation of the concept of presumption of innocence. At some point — before a member of the audience actually fell asleep — Larry would break in to make a pitch for money. As we moved away from one group, I heard a man stage whisper, "She's pretty but someone should tell her to lighten up."

I turned to Larry, who had also heard, and said, "I need a break."

"I'll come and find you."

When he left I found myself near the center of the room. A short, stocky man stood a few feet away staring up at the ceiling. I followed his gaze to the chandelier. It was a sleek metallic thing lit with dozens of silvery candles. The man and I exchanged looks. He smiled.

"At first," he said, "I wondered why Elliot couldn't afford electricity. Then I realized the candles must be much more expensive."

There were faint traces of an English accent in his voice. His face was square and fleshy and showed its age. His was the first truly human visage I'd seen all night.

"It's less conspicuous than burning hundred-dollar bills, I guess."

He laughed. "I heard you introduced, Mr. Rios. My name is Harvey Miller."

"Henry to my friends," I replied, shaking his hand. "Are you part of this crowd?"

"Am I rich? No. I work at the Gay and Lesbian Center on Highland. Elliot's on the board. Do you know about the Center?"

"Sure," I said. "You do good work."

"So do you, I hear." He accepted a glass of champagne from a passing waiter.

I shrugged. "It's my Catholic upbringing. The world's troubles weigh on my heart. *Mea culpa.*"

He sipped from the glass and lowered it. "You seem a bit brittle, Henry."

"This isn't my natural habitat. I was going outside for some air. Join me?"

"I'd like that."

We made our way through the clumps of oversized furnishings and past the squadrons of rented waiters carrying trays of food and drink, to a door that let us out onto an immense patio. We walked to its edge and looked out over the city. Streams of light marked the major boulevards which were crammed with the tail end of rush-hour traffic. The spires of downtown probed the ashen sky. Lights of every color — red, blue, silver, gold — twinkled in the darkness as if the city were an enormous Christmas tree.

I made this comparison to Harvey.

"It is like a Christmas tree," he replied, "but most of the boxes beneath it are empty. For a lot of gay people, anyway."

I looked at him as he finished off the contents of his glass. "What exactly do you do at the Center?"

"I'm a psychologist," he replied, smiling at the city.

"Well," I said, "for a few gay people some boxes, like this house, are crammed full."

"No, not really." He set the glass down on the ledge of the wall. "It's not easy for anyone in this society to be gay."

"I wouldn't waste much sympathy on the rich," I said. "Even compassion has its limits."

He moved a step nearer. "Are you always the life of the party?"

I smiled. "Sorry. Yesterday I was sitting in a filthy little room trying to pry some truth out of Jim Pears and tonight I'm at Valhalla meeting the gay junior league. When the altitude changes this fast I get motion sick."

"Why do you have such a low opinion of us?"

"I don't. It's just that it's not my profession."

"What?"

"Homosexuality."

"No," he said, feigning a smile. "You're a lawyer, right? Never mind that the law oppresses us."

"I thought we were going to be friends, Harvey."

"You can't isolate yourself in your work."

"I'm not trying to," I said. "But Jim Pears is a client, not a cause. If I can save his life, I've done my job."

"And if not?" he asked, leaning against the wall. "Have you still done your job?"

"By my lights," I replied.

He picked up his glass. "I'm disappointed that your lights have such a narrow focus."

I shrugged. "In my work, someone is usually disappointed."

"Good luck," he said and went back inside.

When I went back in, the party was breaking up. I spotted Larry standing with a fat man in a shiny suit. Not an old suit. A shiny one. Larry signalled me to join them. The fat man's face shone like a waxed apple. A fringe of dyed hair was combed low over his forehead. He fidgeted a smile, revealing perfect teeth.

"Henry, this is Sandy Blenheim," Larry said.

I shook Blenheim's hand. It was soft and moist but he compensated with a grip that nearly broke my thumb. Before I could say anything, Blenheim started talking.

"Look, Henry, I'm running a little late." He jabbed his hand into the air, as if to ward off time's passage. "So if we could just get down to business."

"What business is that?"

"I'm an agent. I have a client who's interested in buying the rights to the trial."

"Jim's trial?" I asked.

Blenheim gave three rapid nods.

"Why?"

"To make a movie," Larry interjected.

I looked at Blenheim. "A movie?"

"It's great. The whole set-up. Gay kid exposed. We could take it to the networks and sell it like that." He snapped his pudgy fingers. "We tried talking to the kid's parents but they won't deal. The kid won't even talk to me. So you're our last hope."

"I really don't understand," I said.

Blenheim spread his hands. "We buy your rights, see, and if you can bring the kid and his folks around, that just sweetens the deal. What about it?"

"It's a bit premature, don't you think?" I said. "There hasn't actually been a trial."

"But there will be," Blenheim insisted. "We can give you

twenty," he continued. "Plus, we hire you as the legal consult-ant. You could clean up."

"I'm sorry," I began, "but this conversation is not—"

"Okay," Blenheim said, affably. "I've been around lawyers. You guys are cagey. Tell you what, Henry. Think on it and call me in a couple of weeks. Larry's got my number. See you later."

He turned, waved at someone across the room, and walked away. I looked at Larry. "Have I just been hit by a truck?"

"No, but you might check your wallet."

"What was that all about?"

"Just what the man said," Larry replied. "He wants to make a movie."

"About Jim? That's a little ghoulish, isn't it?"

Larry shrugged. "He gave me a check for five hundred dollars for Jim's defense," he said. "I figured that was worth at least a couple of minutes of your time."

"Okay, he got his two minutes." I looked at Larry; he was pale and seemed tired. "I think we should get you home."

"Fein's invited us for dinner," he replied. "There's no tactful way out."

"Then let's not be tactful," I said.

He began to speak, but then simply nodded. "I am tired," he said.

Fein accepted my excuses with a fixed smile and later when I said good-night he looked at me seemingly without recogni-tion. But the boy who had parked our car remembered me.

"Enjoy yourself?" he asked, opening the car door for me.

Thinking of Fein and Harvey Miller and the fat agent, I said, "It wasn't that kind of party."

— 8 —

I returned to the jail day after day to talk to Jim Pears. We sat at the table in the room with the soiled walls beneath the glaring lights. As far as I knew, he had no other visitors. Jim showed no interest in preparing for the coming trial beyond repeating his stock claim of innocence. He answered my questions with the fewest words possible unless I asked him about the events leading up to the killing. Those he wouldn't answer at all, maintaining loss of memory.

One late afternoon a week after our first interview, I said, "Tell me the last thing you remember about that night."

His blue gaze drifted past my face. "I was at the bar."

"Before Brian got there."

"Yes."

"Do you remember seeing him arrive?"

Jim shook his head. I drew a zero on my legal pad. A blue vein twitched at his temple. His eyes, the same throbbing blue, scanned his fingertips.

"Did Brian ever threaten you?"

He looked up, startled. "No."

"Demand money?"

"No."

"Did you tell him to meet you at the restaurant that night?"

His eyes were terrified. "No."

"Did he tell you he was coming there?"

"No," he replied, drawing a deep breath.

"But once he got there you assumed it was to see you, didn't you?"

"I don't know."

"Don't know what?"

"What I thought." He shifted in his seat.

I drew another zero on the pad. "Tell me about the guy who picked you up the night Brian saw you in the car. Had you ever seen him before?"

"No," he replied.

"What did he look like?"

"That was a long time ago."

"You must remember something," I snapped.

He slumped in his chair. "He was old," he said finally, and added, "Like you."

Ignoring the gibe, I asked, "Was he tall or short?"

"Average, I guess."

"I'm not interested in your guesses. What color was his hair?"

"Dark."

"What about his eyes?"

He was quiet for a moment, then he said, in a voice that was different, almost yearning, "They were blue."

"Like yours?" I asked.

"No, different," he replied in the same voice. He was seeing those eyes.

"Tell me about his eyes," I said, quietly.

"I told you," he replied, the yearning gone. "They were blue."

"How did you end up in his car?"

"He told me to meet him."

"Where?"

"In the lot behind the restaurant."

"Then what happened?"

He stared at me, color creeping up his neck.

"You got in the car and then what happened?"

"We talked." It was almost a question.

"Is that what you were doing when Brian came up to the car, talking?"

He shook his head. "He was — sucking me."

"That's what Brian saw?"

"Yeah."

"What did Brian do?"

"He opened the car door," Jim said, talking quickly, "and yelled 'faggots'. Then he ran back across the lot of the restaurant."

"What did you do?"

"I got out of the car. The guy drove off. I went home."

"Did he tell you his name?"

"No."

I looked at him. No, of course not. Names weren't important.

"Brian threatened to tell your parents," I said. "Did that worry you?"

"Sure," he said, "but—" He stopped himself.

"But what?"

"He didn't."

"The D.A. will say that he didn't because you killed him. What's your explanation?"

"I didn't kill him."

"Why didn't he tell your parents?"

"I don't know," he replied, his voice rising. "Ask him."

"He's dead, Jim. Remember?"

"Yeah, I remember. Why aren't you trying to find the guy that killed him?"

"Why don't you tell me the truth?"

"Fuck you," he replied.

"This isn't getting us anywhere," I observed in a quiet voice. "Are you sleeping better?"

"They give me pills," he said, all the anger gone.

I frowned. I had had Jim examined by a doctor to see what could be done to relieve his anxiety. Apparently the doctor chose a quick fix.

"How often?"

"Three times a day," he said.

"I'd ease up on them," I cautioned.

He shrugged.

"You need anything?"

He shook his head.

"I'll see you tomorrow, then," I said.

His face showed what he thought of the prospect.

□

There was a knock at the door. I got up from the desk and went downstairs. It was Freeman Vidor, whom I had been expecting. I let him in, found him a beer, and led him up to the study.

"Nice place," he commented, sitting on the sofa and looking around the room. He glanced at the piles of paper on the desk. "How's it going?"

"The good news is that there won't be any surprises from the prosecution at trial," I replied. "The bad news is that they don't need any."

He lit a cigarette and looked around for an ashtray. I gave him the cup I had been drinking coffee from.

"What about you?" I asked. "Any surprises?"

He dug into the pocket of his suit and extracted a little note-book. He flipped through pages filled with big, loopy hand-writing. "Maybe."

"Fox?" I asked, setting a fresh notepad on the desk in front of me.

"Uh-huh," he said, and sipped his beer. "There's a private security patrol in the neighborhood where his folks live. Seems about a year ago they started getting complaints about a Peeping Tom. They kept a look-out and, lo and behold, they find Fox in someone's back yard. There's a girl lives there he went to school with. It was just about her bedtime."

"What was his story?"

"He wanted to talk to her," Freeman said, dropping his ciga-rette into the coffee cup and pouring a little beer over it. "Only they caught him with his pants down."

"What?"

"Jerking off. He said he was just taking a piss."

"Anyone press charges?"

"Not in that neighborhood," he said. "Security took him home and told his parents." He belched softly. "Excuse me. There was some other stuff, too," he continued. "Seems like Brian was the neighborhood pervert."

"I'm listening."

Freeman shrugged. "Now these are just rumors," he cautioned. "He spent a lot of time with kids who were younger than him — thirteen, fourteen."

"Boys? Girls?"

"Both," he replied, and finished off the beer. " 'Course, less time with little girls because their folks got kind of suspicious that a high school senior was hanging around them. So mostly he was with the little boys. They thought he was kind of a creep."

"And why is that?"

"A couple of them came over to his house to go swimming when his folks were gone. He gave them some beer and tried to get them to go into the pool naked."

"What happened?"

"They split," he replied and thumbed through the notebook. "After that, they all pretty much avoided him."

"Did they tell their parents?"

He shook his head.

An interesting picture was beginning to develop. I asked, "What about kids his own age? Did he have a girlfriend?"

"Nope," he said. "Didn't go out much with girls. He was kind of a loner except for his computer buddies."

"The stories in the papers make him sound like the most popular kid in his class," I observed.

Freeman lit another cigarette. "The kids didn't write those stories, grown-ups did. They see a young guy, not bad looking, smart enough, killed by some — excuse the expression — faggot. What do you think they're going to make of it?"

"'Golden boy,'" I said, quoting the description from one of the newspaper accounts.

"Yeah," Freeman said, dourly, "Golden boy. Hell," he added, "the only thing golden about that boy's his old man's money. There's a lot of that."

"Rich?"

"Real rich," he replied.

"Then why was he working as a busboy?" I asked.

Freeman shrugged. "Not because he needed the money. His counselor at the school says he told Brian's folks to put him to work. Teach him to fit in — no, what did she say?" He flipped through the notebook. "Learn 'appropriate patterns of socialization,'" he quoted. He grinned at me. "Some homework."

"Did it work? What did they think of him at the restaurant?"

"That he was a lazy little shit," Freeman replied. "They fired him once but his old man got him the job back."

"Speaking of the restaurant, what did you find out about the keys to the service door?"

"There's four copies," he replied. "One for the manager and his two assistants and one they leave at the bar."

"Were they all accounted for?"

"Everyone checks out, except for one. The day manager, a kid named Josh Mandel."

"The prosecutor's star witness," I said.

"That's him."

"No alibi for that night?"

Freeman nodded, slowly. "He says he was out on a date."

"You have trouble with that?"

"Let's just say he don't lie with much conviction."

— 9 —

The next day I called the Yellowtail and learned that Josh Mandel was working the lunch shift. I headed out to Encino at noon on the Hollywood Freeway. October brought cooler weather but no respite from the smog that hung above the city like a soiled, tattered sheet. Hollywood Boulevard looked more derelict than usual, as if the brown air above it were its own gasps and wheezes. The movie money had migrated west, leaving only this elegant carcass mouldering in the steamy autumn sunlight.

The air was clearer in the valley but there was decay here, too; but with none of the fallen-angel glamour of Hollywood. Rather, it lay in the crumbling foundations of jerry-built condominium complexes, condemned drive-ins and bowling alleys, paint blistering from shops on the verge of bankruptcy. The detritus of the good life. It was easy to feel the ghost town just beneath the facade of affluence.

The Yellowtail anchored a small, chic shopping center comprised of clothing boutiques and specialty food stores, white stucco walls, covered walkways, tiled roofs, murmuring fountains, and grass the color of new money. I pulled into the parking lot beside the restaurant and walked around to the entrance. Heavy paneled doors led into a sunlit anteroom. A blonde girl stood at a podium with a phone pressed to her ear. She looked at me, smiled meaninglessly, and continued her conversation.

I walked to the edge of the anteroom. The restaurant was basically a big rectangular room with two smaller rooms off the main floor. The first of these, nearest to where I stood, was the bar. The other, only distantly visible, seemed to be a smaller dining room. The entire place was painted in shades of pink and white and gray. Behind the bar there was an aquarium in which exotic fish fluttered through blue-green water like shards of an aquatic rainbow.

There were carnations in crystal vases on each table. Moody abstracts hung from the walls. Light streamed in from a bank of tall, narrow windows on the wall opposite the bar. The windows faced an interior courtyard, flowerbeds, and a fountain in the shape of a lion's head. Above the din of expense-account conversation I heard a bit of Vivaldi. The waiters were as handsome as the room they served. They seemed college-age or slightly older, most of them blond, wearing khaki trousers, blue button-down shirts, sleeves rolled to the elbows, red silk ties. The busboys were similarly dressed but without ties. They swept across the tiled floor like ambulatory mannequins.

"Excuse me, are you waiting for someone?" It was the girl at the podium. I looked at her. She was very nearly pretty but for the spoiled twist of her lips.

"I'd like to see Josh Mandel."

"Are you a salesman?" she asked, already looking beyond me to a couple just leaving.

"No, I'm Jim Pears's lawyer."

Her eyes focused on me. Without a word, she picked up the phone and pressed two numbers. There was a quick, sotto voce conversation and when she put the phone down she said, "He asked for you to wait for him in the bar."

"Fine. By the way, is Andrea Lew working today?"

The girl said, "She quit."

"Do you know how I can reach her?"

"No," she said in a tone she probably practiced on her boyfriend.

"Thanks for your help," I replied, and felt her eyes on my back as I made my way to the bar. I found an empty bar stool and ordered a Calistoga water. Andrea Lew was right; it was impossible for anyone to enter the restaurant without being seen from the bar. Assuming, of course, that someone was watching.

I was about to ask the bartender about Andrea when I heard someone say, "Mr. Rios?"

I looked up at the dark-haired boy who had spoken. "You're Josh," I said, recognizing him from court.

He nodded. In court he had seemed older. Now I saw he was very young, two or three years out of his teens, and trying to conceal the fact. The round horn-rimmed glasses didn't help. They only called attention to green-brown eyes that had the bright sheen of true innocence. His hair was a mass of black curls restrained by a shiny mousse. He had a delicate, bony face, a long nose, a wide strong mouth and the smooth skin of a child. "Why don't we go down to my office," he said, and I was suddenly aware that we had been staring at each other.

"You mind showing me around the place first?" I asked, stepping down from the bar stool. I was about an inch taller than he.

He frowned but nodded. "You've already seen all this," he said, jutting his chin at the dining room. "I'll show you the back."

We made our way across the big room and pushed through swinging double doors.

"This is the waiter's station," he told me. We were in a narrow room. The kitchen was visible over a counter through a rectangular window on which the cooks placed orders as they were ready and clanged a bell to alert the waiters. In one corner was a metal rack with four plastic tubs filled with dirty dishes. A busboy took the top tub and carried it out through another door behind us. Pots of coffee bubbled on the counter. Cupboards held coffee cups, glasses, napkins, and cutlery. One of the blond waiters walked in, lit a cigarette and smoked furiously.

"Put it out, Timmy," Josh said as we passed through the door where the busboy had gone and stood at the top of a corridor that terminated at the back door. Josh walked toward it. I followed.

"Dishwasher," he said, stopping in front of a small room where a slender black man wearing a hair net pushed a rack of dishes into an immense machine.

We walked back a little farther. "Employees' locker room," Josh said. There were three rows of lockers against a wall. Opposite the lockers were two doors, marked men and women. A bench completed the decor. "This is where we change for work," he said.

We went back into the corridor.

"Back door," he said, pointing.

I looked at the door and realized, for the first time, that the lock which Andrea Lew had talked about was an interior lock. Inspecting it further I saw that it could not be unlocked from outside at all but only from within. I asked Josh about it.

"It's for security," he replied. "It can't be picked from outside."

"You keep it unlocked during the day?"

"Uh-huh, for deliveries. Night manager locks it up when the kitchen closes at ten."

"So if anyone was back here after ten he'd need a key to get out?"

"Uh-huh," he said.

"But there's a key at the bar."

He looked at me and blinked. "Yeah, for emergencies."

"Show me the cellar," I said.

I followed him back down the corridor and around the front of the walk-in refrigerator. We passed briefly through the kitchen and then went down a rickety flight of stairs into the cellar. We stood in a big, dark room that had a damp, fruity smell. Behind locked wooden screens were hundreds of bottles of wine. The room was otherwise bare. He showed me two smaller rooms adjacent to each other. The door to one of them was open, revealing a cluttered desk. The door to the other was closed.

"That's where they found Jim," he said. "You want to go in?" His voice indicated clearly that he didn't.

"Maybe later," I said, giving him a break.

We went into his office. He sat in a battered swivel chair behind a desk made of a thick slab of glass supported by metal sawhorses. There was a phone on the wall, its lights flashing.

He closed a ledger on the desk before him and offered me a cup of coffee. I declined.

"How's Jim?" he asked.

"Surviving."

"I'm really sorry about what happened," he said, defensively. "They told me I had to testify."

"Of course you did," I said soothingly. "You seem pretty young to be managing this place."

"I'm twenty-two," he protested, and must have caught my smile. "I usually just manage the floor but Mark — he's the head guy — he's out sick today."

"Have you worked here long?"

"Six years. I started as a busboy."

"You go to school?"

He picked up a paper clip. "Two years at UCLA. I dropped out."

"Why?"

He flattened out the paper clip. "Is that important?"

"I won't know until you tell me."

He set the paper clip aside. "I didn't know what I was doing there," he said. "I never was much for school."

I accepted this, for the moment. "What was Jim like to work with?"

He was visibly relieved by the change of subject. "He was a hard worker," Josh said. "Reliable."

"You ever see him outside of work?"

He shook his head and picked up a pencil.

"Were you surprised to find out he was gay?"

Our eyes caught. "What do you mean?"

"Didn't Brian tell you Jim was gay?"

"Yes."

"Did you believe him?"

He put the pencil down. "Yes."

"Why?"

He looked at the desk. "I don't know. I just did."

I let his answer.hang in the air. He picked up the paper clip again.

"And later you heard Brian threaten to tell Jim's parents."

"It wasn't exactly like that," he said, softly.

"No?"

"It was more — like a joke," he said, raising his head slowly. "Brian said something like, 'You want your mama to know you suck cock?' like the way little kids insult each other."

"And Jim? Did he know it was a joke?"

"I think so," he replied. "He kind of laughed and said, 'I'll kill you first.'"

"Where did this happen?"

"The locker room. We were all changing for work."

"This was the only time you ever heard them say anything to each other like this?"

"Yes," he said, and bit his lower lip.

"You know, Josh," I said, "this sounds entirely different than it did when you testified at the prelim."

"I told the prosecutor but he kept saying that Jim really meant it because, you know, he did kill Brian. I guess he convinced me."

"Do you think Jim killed Brian?" I asked.

"That's what they say. All the evidence looks pretty bad for Jim."

"Do you think he did it?" I asked again.

Josh took off his glasses and cleaned them with his handkerchief. "I don't know," he said, finally.

"Can you think of anyone else who would have a reason to kill Brian Fox?"

He shook his head quickly.

"Where were you the night he was killed?"

He looked shocked. "On a date."

I looked at him until he looked away. He was lying. "Who with?"

Recovering himself he said, "The D.A. said I don't have to talk to you."

"But you are going to have to testify again," I said.

"I'll tell the truth," he replied, his face coloring. It was useless to push him.

"You won't have any choice, Josh," I said. I wrote Larry's number on a slip of paper. "If you want to talk later you can reach me here."

He looked at the paper as if it were a bomb, but took it and slipped it into his pocket.

□

Larry's car was in the driveway though it was only two-thirty. That worried me. Except for a certain gauntness, Larry gave no sign of being gravely ill, but his condition was never far from my mind. I knew it preoccupied Larry, too. Sometimes he became very still and remote. It actually seemed as if some part of him were gone. When I mentioned it, he smiled and said he was practicing levitation. What he was actually doing, I think, was practicing dying.

I found him in his study on the phone. He saw me and motioned me to sit down.

"Sandy," he said to his caller, "you really can do better than Rogers, Stone."

I recognized this as the name of a well-known entertainment law firm. Larry put on his patient face. I could hear his caller's voice across the room.

"That's true," Larry said, "but I'm not available." He listened. "I know you think he walks on water, Sandy, but the guy's a one-season sensation. Next year you'll be pushing someone else." He picked up a pen and started to doodle on a legal pad. "Look," he said finally, "I'll think about it, and get back to you. No, I really will think about it. What? Yeah, he's right here." He pushed the mute button on the phone and said, "It's Sandy Blenheim. He wants to talk to you."

"The fat guy at Fein's party?"

Larry nodded. "The one who wants to make you a star."

Reluctantly, I took the phone. "Hello, this is Henry Rios."

"Henry," Blenheim said, all oily affability. "You think about my proposal?"

"No, not really. I haven't had much time."

There was a disappointed silence at his end of the line. "What is it, Henry? The money?"

"Look, Mr. Blenheim ... "

"Sandy."

"Sandy. I don't think this is going to make a good movie."

"There's a lot of kids out there in Jim's position," Blenheim said. "Kids in the closet. Kids getting picked on. This picture could show them there's a right way to come out and a wrong way. You know what I'm saying?"

I shot a glance at Larry. He smiled. "Sure, I understand," I said. "But this isn't the right—" I searched for the word. "—vehicle," I said.

Larry nodded approvingly.

"Come on, you've talked to the kid. You know what's going through his head. That's the good stuff. Like how did he feel when he pulled the trigger—"

I cut him off. "Actually, he doesn't remember."

"What do you mean he doesn't remember?"

"Just what I said," I replied, "and I've really told you more than I should but it's just so you know that this isn't the story you think it is."

"Maybe if we talked some more," he suggested.

"I'm sorry," I replied. "It wouldn't serve any purpose. Do you want to talk to Larry?"

"Yeah, put him back on."

I handed the phone to Larry. "It's for you."

"Yes, Sandy," he said. I heard the angry buzz of Blenheim's voice complaining about my intransigence. Larry broke in and said, "He doesn't want more money, Sandy. He wants to try his case in peace." More angry buzzing. "Well," Larry said, shortly, "I think it's called integrity. You might look it up in the dictionary." There was a click on the other end. "If you can spell it," Larry added.

"I didn't mean for him to get mad at you, too," I said.

Larry put the phone down. "Big finishes are a way of life around here. He'll be over it by tomorrow."

"You're home early."

He lit a cigarette. "Yeah. I was having a terrible day — about the two millionth since I passed the bar, and then it occurred to me, what the hell am I doing?" He smiled and drew on his cigarette. "I'm not into terrible days anymore."

"Maybe you should just quit."

"And do what, die?" He looked at me and smirked. "Was that tactless?"

"Yes," I replied. "A sure sign you're getting better."

"Did you see the waiter?" Larry asked, putting out his cigarette. I noticed that he had only smoked it half-way down.

"Yeah."

"And was he a rabid queer-baiter?"

"Didn't seem the type," I said, thinking of Josh Mandel's eyes. "I could be wrong, of course. He did lie to me."

"About anything important?"

"It was about what he was doing the night Brian was killed," I replied. "I don't know yet if that's important. On the other hand, I've figured out why Jim insists he didn't kill Brian Fox."

"Why?" Larry asked.

"Because they were lovers."

— 10 —

"Really?" His eyebrows flicked upwards.

I told him what I had learned about Brian Fox's sexual escapades. A penchant for voyeurism, and budding pedophilia was of a different order than fumbling in the back seat with more-or-less willing partners of the same age. Yet how different were these activities from Jim's excursions into bathrooms and parks? To me, they revealed a kind of sexual despair. I could understand that in Jim's case; he was gay and his fear drove him underground. But what about Brian Fox? Maybe it didn't matter. What was important was that Brian was unusually sensitive to Jim's sexual secret. My guess was that what drew Brian to Jim was not antipathy as much as fascination — one sexual loner's recognition of another.

"I don't think Brian followed Jim out into the parking lot because he wanted to embarrass him," I said. "I think he wanted to know for sure whether Jim was gay."

"Are you saying Brian was gay, too?" Larry asked.

"God, I hope not. Let's just say he was—"

"A pervert?"

"That'll do for now."

"That's the pot calling the kettle beige."

I walked to the window and looked past the terraced garden to the shimmering lake. "Jury trials demand a sacrifice," I said. "And if it's not going to be Jim, it has to be Brian."

"You still haven't explained why you think they were lovers."

"The first thing is why Brian didn't tell anyone about Jim."

"Didn't he tell Josh Mandel?"

"But not Jim's parents," I replied. "The obvious reason seemed to be blackmail, but there's a limit to how much you can extort from an eighteen-year-old busboy."

"To how much money," Larry said, revelation in his voice.

"Exactly. But the other thing that might've interested Brian was sex. Sex on demand."

"You think it didn't matter to him that it was another guy?"

"A blow job is a blow job is a blow job."

"*Pace* Gertrude Stein," Larry murmured and leaned back into his chair. "You said lovers, Henry. This scenario is not my idea of a romance."

"Agreed, but then — what did Auden say — 'The desires of the heart are as crooked as the corkscrew.' Josh Mandel described the scene where Jim supposedly threatened to kill Brian." I related Josh's version from that afternoon.

"Puts things in a different light," Larry said, extracting a cigarette from his pack of Kents.

"Doesn't it," I agreed. "It sounds like post-coital banter."

"Who have you been sleeping with?"

"You know what I mean."

Larry lit the Kent. He blew out a jet of smoke and nodded. "You think some affection developed between those two."

"It adds up."

"So am I to infer that Jim didn't kill Brian?" Larry asked, tapping ash into a crystal ashtray.

"No, the evidence is inescapable. It only explains why he can't bring himself to admit it. He didn't hate Brian."

"Then why kill him?"

"It was still blackmail," I said. "Brian had power over Jim. At some point Jim must have realized that Brian was using him and would go on using him whether Jim consented or not."

"That must've been hard if he cared at all about Brian."

"And it added to his guilt about being gay. Being gay meant being a victim."

Larry put out the cigarette and rose from behind his desk. "What are you going to do?"

"Go back to Jim. Let him know that I know."

"I suppose you have to," Larry said, gathering his cigarettes.

"You think I shouldn't?"

Larry shrugged. "He hasn't told you because he wanted to keep it a secret. Think of his pride."

"That's a luxury he can't afford," I replied.

□

Jim came out and sat at the table, focusing on my left ear. His face was slack and tired.

"Were you asleep?" I asked.

"Who can sleep around here," he muttered.

"The tranquilizers don't help?"

His shrug terminated that line of conversation.

"I wanted to talk to you about Brian."

"Okay," he said, indifferently.

The indifference stung. "You were lovers," I said.

He gave me a hard look. "Guys don't love each other," he said.

"But you had sex with him."

His face colored but he didn't look away. "He wanted it," he said slowly.

"Did you?"

His narrow fingers raked his hair.

"Was having sex with him the price Brian charged for not telling your parents about you?"

He nodded. He looked at me again, his childishness gone. "Brian always wanted to make it with me," he said, knowingly. "He just needed a reason—"

"An excuse, you mean."

"—so he wouldn't have to think he was a faggot."

"How did you feel about being with him?" I asked.

"I don't know," he said, out of the side of his mouth. "Sometimes he was a jerk about it. Sometimes it was — okay."

"Did you like him?"

"Once when his parents were gone, we slept at his house," Jim said. "That was really nice, in a bed and everything."

"Where did you usually meet Brian for sex?"

"His car," Jim said. "The park. The locker room at the restaurant."

"The wine cellar?"

His eyes showed fear.

"Was that why he was there that night?"

"I don't know why he was there," Jim said. His voice trembled.

"But you assumed that's why he was there," I said. "Didn't you?"

After a moment's hesitation he said, "Yeah."

"Did Brian like you as much as you liked him?" I asked quietly.

He shook his head slowly, surprise in his face. "He never stopped calling me a faggot when other guys were around. Even after we made it. He told Josh Mandel about me."

"And you still liked him?" I continued.

"He was different when we were alone," Jim said, almost mournfully. He sounded less like the jilted lover than the slightly oddball child other children avoid; the mousy-haired boy lingering at the edge of the playing field watching a game he was never asked to play.

"So," I said, in a matter-of-fact voice, "one part of you really liked him and another part of you hated him because he was using you, Jim. Isn't that how it was?"

He opened his mouth but nothing came out. He nodded.

"Part of you loved him—" I waited, but he didn't react. "And part of you wanted—"

As if continuing a different conversation, he broke in, "Everything was so fucked up. I was tired." I heard the exhaustion pouring out from a deep place. "I wanted to kill—"

"Brian," I said.

"Myself," he replied. "I wanted to kill myself. Not Brian. I didn't kill Brian."

"But Brian's the one who's dead, Jim."

"No," he said, his face closing. "You think I killed him, but I didn't. I wanted to kill myself."

"That's what you wanted, Jim, but think about it," I said,

quickly. "Wanting to kill anyone means that there's violence inside of you. You can't always control that violence or direct it the way you planned. It's like a fire, Jim."

He was shaking his head violently, and his body trembled. "No, no, no," he said. "It wasn't me. I swear it wasn't."

"Think back, Jim. Try to remember that night."

"I don't remember," he said in a gust.

"You do remember," I said. "You have to, Jim."

His body buckled and then he started to scream. The guard ran up behind and restrained him, looking at me with amazement. As quickly as he had started, Jim stopped and slumped forward. Tears and snot ran down his face. He lifted his face and looked at me with such hatred that I felt my face burn.

"You're like everyone else," he said. "You want me to say I killed him. To hell with you." To the guard he said, "Get me out of here."

"We have to talk," I said.

"No more talking. You're not my lawyer anymore."

He jerked up out of the chair. The guard looked at me, seeking direction.

"Okay, Jim. I'll be back tomorrow."

"I won't be here," Jim Pears said.

□

A phone was ringing.

I opened my eyes and tumbled out of bed, hurrying to pick the phone up before it woke Larry.

"Hello," I said, shaking from the chill.

A drunken male voice slurred my name.

"Yes, this is Henry. Who is this?"

"I know who killed Brian whatsisname," the voice continued.

I sat down at the desk. "Who are you?"

"It's not important," he said. "It wasn't that Pears kid. I'll tell you that much."

I was trying to clear my head and decide whether this was a crank call. I still wasn't sure.

"Were you at the bar that night?" I asked.

"Not me. Shit, you wouldn't catch me dead in the valley," he said and chuckled.

"Then how do you know?"

"I saw you on the news," he said. "You're kinda cute, Henry. You gotta lover?"

"Tell me about Brian Fox."

I heard bar noises in the background and then the line went dead.

I put the phone down. If it was a crank call, the caller had gone to a lot of trouble to find me. He would have had to call my office up north to get Larry's phone number. Unless he already had it. Josh Mandel? As I tried to reconstruct the voice, the phone rang again. I picked it up.

"Hello," I said, quickly.

"Mr. Rios?" It was a different voice, also male but not drunk.

"Yeah. Who am I talking to?"

"This is Deputy Isbel down at county jail," he said. "We got a bad situation here with Jim Pears."

"What happened?"

"Seems like he overdosed."

I stared at my faint reflection in the black window. "Is he dead?" I watched myself ask.

"No," the deputy replied cautiously. "They took him down to county hospital. Thought you'd want to know."

"Did you call his parents?"

"His dad answered," the deputy said, grimly. "Thanked me and hung up before I could tell him where the boy was."

"I see," I replied. "Where's the hospital if I'm coming from Silver Lake?"

I scrawled the directions on the back of an envelope and hung up. In the bathroom, I splashed water on my face, subdued my hair, rinsed my mouth, and dressed. I crept down the stairs. Just as I was closing the front door behind me, I heard the phone ring again. By the time I got to it, the caller had hung up.

— **11** —

Jim was still alive at daybreak. His doctor set her breakfast tray on the table in the hospital cafeteria where I had been waiting for her. She took a bite of scrambled eggs and made a face.

"They should make hospital cooks take the Hippocratic oath," she said. "'First, do no harm.' That part."

I smiled, not too convincingly to judge from her expression. Her face was the color of exhaustion. She turned her attention to her meal, and ate with complete concentration as if taking a test. When she lifted her head, she looked almost relieved to be done with it.

"How are you feeling?" she asked.

I smiled again, this time genuinely. No matter how casually a doctor asked, this question always sounded like an accusation to me.

"I'm tired," I replied.

She nodded understandingly. "Go home."

"If he's all right."

Her narrow, studious face tensed a bit. "I didn't say that."

"No," I agreed, "you didn't."

"He's alive, Henry, but not all right." She rubbed her eyes. "He was unconscious for a long time, not breathing well. There's brain damage. How did he get those barbituates in jail?"

"They were prescribed," I answered. "To relieve anxiety. He must have stockpiled them."

"If they'd found him five minutes later, he'd be dead."

"It seems that was his plan." In my head I heard him telling me that he wouldn't be at the jail when I returned to see him.

According to the guards who'd brought him into the hospital, one of Jim's cellmates had been awakened by a gurgling noise. It was Jim, choking on his own vomit.

"You never said what he was in for," the doctor said.

"Murder," I replied.

"That little guy?"

"Yes," I said. He had also told me that he had wanted to kill himself, not Brian. Well, maybe he killed part of himself when he killed Brian. He decided to finish the job. Thanks to me.

She curled her elegant fingers around a chipped coffee mug. "Well, he did manage to do a lot of damage to himself, so I guess murder's not impossible."

"Will he live?"

"Parts of him." She wore a thin gold wedding band. She saw me notice it and said, "You were one of the lawyers on that sodomy case a couple of years back."

"I'm surprised you remember."

"I recognized your name as soon as you told me. You're his lawyer, or what?"

"His lawyer," I said, shaking the grounds at the bottom of my coffee cup.

"No parents?"

"He has parents," I said, setting the cup down. "They couldn't be bothered."

"That's rough," she said, blinking the tiredness from her eyes. She studied me. "Was his situation so bad?"

I nodded. "He got backed into a corner. I helped put him there."

"Working in emergency," she said, "I see a lot of suicide attempts. The ones who survive, they didn't mean to succeed." She pushed her tray away. "The ones who don't make it — it's not that they give up, Henry. They fight, but they fight to die. That's what Jim's doing. You can murder someone, but you can't make him kill himself. You understand?"

I studied the pattern of the grounds at the bottom of my cup. "Yes," I said, lifting my tired eyes to hers.

"Go home," she said. "I'll call you if anything happens."

□

It was cold and gray outside the hospital. The sun was like a circle of ice, lightening the sky around it. The silvery towers of downtown shimmered through the morning mist. In this weather the palm trees seemed wildly incongruous, like tattered banners of summer.

I had read, years ago, of the Japanese poet who commented upon suicide, "A silent death is an endless word." Should I read Jim's attempt to kill himself as a reproach, as release, as an admission of guilt? Of love? I could understand why he did it but I didn't approve. It was the drama that disturbed me. The most basic rule of survival is to wait things out. It was a rule Jim was too young to have learned. With almost twenty years on him, I knew that the great passions — love, fear, hope, terror — merge with the clutter of the day-to-day, and become part of it. A truer symbol of justice than the blindfolded goddess was a clock.

A clock was ticking in the kitchen of Larry's house as I let myself in. He was sitting at the table with a cup of coffee in front of him. He looked up when I entered.

"I heard your car when you left," he said. "That was six hours ago."

"You've been awake since?"

"Off and on," he replied. "It's Jim, isn't it?"

"He tried to kill himself," I said, sitting down.

In a gray voice, Larry asked, "Is he dead?"

"No. He's in a coma."

"How did it happen?"

I explained.

Larry raised the cup to his lips without drinking. The robe he wore fell away, revealing his thin, hairless chest, the skin as mottled as an autumn apple. A few sparse white hairs grew at the base of his neck. His face showed nothing of what he felt but the white hairs trembled.

"How stupid," he muttered. "What a stupid thing to do."

"He was afraid," I said.

"Well I know a few things about fear," Larry snapped. He shut his eyes for a moment. When he opened them he said, "I'm sorry I said that."

"Who better?"

"No," he shook his head. "It's not the same at all. I've had my life, but to throw it all away at eighteen..." He lifted his fingers from the table in a gesture of bewilderment.

"If you can't imagine the future," I said, "it must not seem like you're throwing much away."

Larry nodded. "You'll have to do something about the trial."

"I'll ask for a dismissal."

"Then what?"

"I suppose he'll revert to the custody of his parents."

Larry frowned. "The perfect son at last."

I went upstairs to get some sleep. As I undressed I remembered the call I received the night before. I called my office and reached my secretary. I asked whether anyone had requested my number in the last day or so.

She went through the telephone log. There had been someone, a man named King who had insisted on getting my number in Los Angeles. The name meant nothing to me. I thanked her and hung up.

I got into the rumpled bed, naked between the cold sheets. Outside, a bird cawed. Inside, there was silence. I closed my eyes and slept a long, black sleep.

□

Three days later I was back in court. The press was out in full force. Pisano, the D.A., told the court he would not dismiss the charges against Jim Pears as long as Jim remained alive. He put Lillian Fox on the witness stand. She demanded that the prosecution proceed. I informed Judge Ryan that Jim had suffered permanent, catastrophic brain damage and was unlikely ever to revive. I asked the judge to dismiss the charges on her own motion, as the law permitted, in the interests of justice. However, as she had just finished pointing out, those interests were complex.

"Your Honor," I said, "the medical evidence is that my client is, for all intents and purposes, dead. I don't see what more could be accomplished by hounding him to the grave."

Pisano was on his feet. "The medical evidence is not conclusive," he said.

"It's as conclusive as it's going to get," I snapped. "Jim Pears isn't going to get much deader, short of driving a stake through his heart."

"So dramatic," Pisano said, mockingly.

"You're just trying to squeeze another headline from this, aren't you?"

The judge broke in. "Gentlemen, some restraint."

"Speaking of restraints," I said, angry now, "my client's wrist is handcuffed to the railing of his hospital bed. Do the police really think he's going to rise up and go on a crime spree? This entire hearing is ghoulish. Regardless of what Jim is charged with, what he may or may not have done, we've reached a point where simple decency demands that this matter be ended."

"Is that true about the handcuffs?" the judge asked.

"Yes," I replied.

"It's standard operating procedure," Pisano put in, in his best bureaucratic drone.

"Even so," Judge Ryan said to him, "it's a little gratuitous, counsel, don't you think?"

"Not at all," he replied.

"The motion, Judge," I said, "is pending."

"Thank you, I'm aware of that," she replied, sharply. Then, looking down at some papers before her, she said, "This matter is scheduled for trial in four weeks. I will continue it until that date for a status hearing. In the meantime, the defendant's motion to dismiss is denied without prejudice to renew it at that point. That's all, gentlemen." She rose swiftly and departed the bench.

I turned to Pisano. "Think the streets are safer now?" I demanded.

He capped the pen he had taken notes with. "This isn't personal, Henry. It's business. Learn that and you'll live a lot longer."

"Calling it business doesn't make it right."

He smiled faintly. "You shouldn't be a lawyer, Henry. You should be God." He walked away to talk to Lillian Fox who was hissing his name behind us.

"Henry?"

It was Sharon Hart, looking like a giant bumblebee in a black suit and a yellow silk blouse.

"Hello, Sharon. I didn't see you come in," I said, closing my briefcase.

"I slipped in halfway through," she said. "I'm in trial next door."

"How's it going?" I asked without real interest.

She shrugged. "My guy's found Jesus."

I smiled, in spite of myself. "What?"

"He admits everything but says that Jesus has forgiven him and the jury should, too."

"Think they'll buy it?"

She grinned. "Not Mrs. Kohn," she said. "Juror number six. You were real good, just now."

"Didn't seem to help."

"Don't blame yourself, or Pat Ryan. Judges are elected, too, and if you're black and a woman someone's always gunning for you. She's got to be careful."

"The fact that the lynch mob has the franchise, instead of a rope and a tree, doesn't make this justice. She should understand that."

"I'm sure she does," Sharon said, frowning. "Trust me, she'll do the right thing. Anyway, it's not like Jim's innocent."

"At this point his guilt or innocence is irrelevant," I replied. "He's removed himself from the court's jurisdiction."

"Tough way to do it," she commented, sticking an unlit cigarette into the side of her mouth. The bailiff cleared his throat censoriously. The cigarette went back into her pocket.

"But effective," I replied.

"Yeah," she said. "I've got a couple of clients I'd like to tell to kill themselves."

I shook my head.

"I've got to get back to my trial," she said, and looked at me steadily. "But there's one thing I've got to ask you. Do you think Jim killed Brian Fox?"

"Yes," I replied, without hesitation. "I do."

She looked relieved. "Well, I guess this is goodbye," she said, and stuck her hand out at me.

I shook it. "Goodbye, Sharon."

"Good luck," she replied. I watched her leave the courtroom. I began to follow but remembered the press outside. In no mood for further combat, I slipped out through the back.

□

Larry drove me to the airport and pulled up in front of the Air California terminal. We got out and I took my things from the trunk.

"You're sure you don't want me to see you off inside?" he asked.

"I'm sure," I replied. We looked at each other. "You wanted me to balance the accounts. I didn't do it, did I?"

Larry looked worn and frail. "I guess Jim showed us that people aren't numbers."

"No," I agreed. "I'll be back in a month."

"Until then."

We embraced and he kissed my cheek. I stood at the curb and watched his Jaguar melt into the frantic Friday afternoon traffic.

On the plane I thought about the loose ends: a drunken phone call from someone who claimed Jim wasn't the killer, Jim's own insistence that he hadn't done it, the fact that Jim and Brian had been something akin to lovers, and Josh Mandel's obvious lie about where he had been the night of the murder. Grist for speculation but hardly enough to take to the jury. Not even enough to change my own mind, really. Jim Pears had killed Brian Fox. That much was inescapable. And yet...

I looked out the window. The sea was white with light, an enormous blankness beneath a gentle autumn sky.

— 12 —

On Monday, December first, I found myself back in the court-room of Patricia Ryan where the case of People versus Pears was about to end — not with a bang, but a whimper. The previous week I had worked out an arrangement allowing the D.A. to designate a neurologist to examine Jim for the purpose of assessing his chances of recovery. The doctor, a sandy-haired man with a vague air about him, sat beside the prosecutor, a young woman named Laura Wyle, the third prosecutor I had dealt with in the past month. The case was now of such low priority that it had trickled down through the ranks to the most junior member of the D.A.'s homicide unit.

It was as cold in the court as it was outside in the rainy streets, the result, I was told, of the heat having been off over the weekend. The bailiff wore a parka over his tan uniform and the court reporter sat with her hands beneath her legs while we waited for the judge to take the bench. The only other people in the court were a middle-aged couple, the man very tall and the woman very short. Jim's parents. Walter Pears wore a black suit, a brilliantly white shirt and a dark blue tie. Light gleamed off the lenses of his wire-rimmed glasses. His long, stern face was set in a look of sour distaste that I associated with religious fanatics and tax lawyers; Walter Pears was both. His wife was, for all intents and purposes, invisible. Even now, looking at her, I was more aware of the color of her dress — an unflattering shade of green — than her face. They were here to reclaim their son. Poor Jim, I thought again, turning away from them. The bailiff stood up and said, "All rise."

Patricia Ryan emerged from her chambers, seated herself and said, "Good morning, ladies and gentlemen."

We bid her good morning. The reporter started to click away.

"People versus Pears," the judge said. "Let the record reflect that the parties are represented but Mr. Pears is not present." She shuffled some papers. "I have received a medical report in this case by a Dr. Connor—"

"Uh, present," the doctor said.

"Yes, hello, Doctor," the judge said. "From what I gather it is your conclusion that Jim Pears suffers from permanent and irreversible brain damage, is that right?"

Doctor Connor drew himself up and surveyed the room as if he had just awakened in Oz. He saw me and blinked furiously.

"Doctor," the judge said.

"Right," he said. "Uh, yes, Your Honor. Did you say something?"

In a voice of practiced patience, she repeated her original question.

Connor's arms jerked up to his sides and backwards as if pulled by wires. "That's kind of the village idiot explanation," he said, cheerfully.

Judge Ryan squinted and said coldly, "Doctor, I'd like you to answer my question, not assess my intelligence."

The D.A. tugged at Connor's coat. He leaned over and she whispered, fiercely, into his ear. He jerked upright and said, "The answer is yes." He plopped back into his chair.

"Thank you," she said. "Now, it's my understanding that the People wish to make a motion pursuant to Penal Code section 1385."

Laura Wyle stood up. "In view of the unlikelihood that James Pears will ever be fit to stand trial, the People move to dismiss the action in the interests of justice."

"Mr. Rios?"

"No objection, Your Honor."

"Motion granted. The action is dismissed. Mr. Pears is remanded to the custody of his parents. Are they in court?"

"Yes, Your Honor," I said, rising. I turned to the gallery.

Sometime during Connor's disquisition Josh Mandel had entered the courtroom and now sat behind me. Surprised, I wondered why the D.A. had ordered him in. "Mr. and Mrs. Pears are present."

"I am ordering Jim's release," she said to them. "You'll have to make arrangements to move him through the sheriff's office. My clerk will assist you."

Walter Pears rose, all six-foot-six of him. "Thank you," he bellowed, mournfully.

"Court is in recess," Patricia Ryan said. "Thank you for being here, Mr. Rios."

"My pleasure."

She smiled charmingly and left the bench. I turned to Laura Wyle. "You have a witness here," I observed.

She looked around. "Where?"

"Josh Mandel."

"I didn't tell him to be here," she replied.

Connor came around and said, loudly, "Can I go now? I have appointments all morning."

"Certainly," she said. "Thank you."

"A waste of my time," he muttered, and pushed his way past the railing and out of the court.

I raised a sympathetic eyebrow at the D.A.

"He's a real ass, isn't he," she said. "Well, excuse me, Henry. Lillian Fox is upstairs in my office having hysterics."

"My sympathies," I said.

Walter Pears came up to the railing, leaned over and said, "Mr. Rios, if I might have a word with you? Privately."

I looked at him. "Sure. Now?"

"If you please."

"There's a small conference room just outside the courtroom," I said. "I'll be there in a minute."

"Yes, that'll do," he said, as if bestowing a favor.

I turned around in my chair. Josh Mandel was looking directly at me. "Hello, Josh."

"Hi," he said. Today he wore a yellow rain slicker over jeans and a red crew neck sweater. Not witness apparel, I thought.

"You came in for the last act?"

"Can I talk to you?"

"I think the Pears have first dibs. Can you stick around?"

He shook his head. "I've got to get to Encino."

"You want to tell me what it's about?" I asked, standing up and straightening my coat.

"It's kind of personal." He was forcing himself to keep his eyes on me.

"Is it about Jim?"

"Sort of," he said, now standing too. The railing separated us by a few inches. "I don't think he killed Brian."

"You have some evidence?"

"Maybe. I'm not sure — look, can I see you tonight?"

"I have plans, I'm afraid."

His face was adamant. "It doesn't matter when. I'll be home all night."

"Give me your number," I said, after a moment's hesitation. "I'll call you."

"Okay." He pulled out his wallet and extracted a bank deposit slip, jotting his number on the back. "It's in Hollywood," he said.

"I'll call," I said, accepting the paper.

"Thanks," he said, and stuck his hand out. I shook it. I watched him go. Handsome kid, I thought, and felt disloyal to Jim for having thought it.

□

Walter Pears folded his hands in front of him. They were big hands with stubby, hairy fingers. He wore a heavy gold band on one finger and what looked like a high school graduation ring on another. His wife, introduced as either Leona or Mona, sat a few inches behind him as watchful as a little bird. I sat down in the only other chair in the room and closed the door behind me.

I waited for Pears to speak.

"As I told you earlier," Pears began after a few uncomfortable seconds, "I am also a lawyer. A tax specialist."

"Yes," I replied. "You told me."

"I know nothing of litigation."

It was clear that he expected congratulations.

"Well, some lawyers just aren't cut out for it," I said.

A bit of color crept into his neck. "That's not precisely why I introduce the subject."

"Do I get three guesses or are you going to tell me?"

He straightened himself in his chair. "I take exception to your tone."

"You're wasting my time," I replied. "And, as one lawyer to another, you know what billing rates are like these days."

For a moment he simply stared at me while his knuckles went white. Then he cleared his throat and said, "My wife and I wish to file a suit against the county. That is, I believe, the proper governmental entity responsible for the maintenance and operation of the jail."

"That's right," I said, outrage beginning to flicker in some dim corner of my brain. "What cause of action do you have against the county?"

"I have undertaken a preliminary investigation of the circumstances surrounding my son's suicide attempt," he announced. "It appears that the medication he took was prescribed to him by a physician at the jail."

"There's no mystery about that."

"Then you will agree that the authorities at the jail failed to monitor whether James was, in fact, taking that medication when it was given to him?"

"I wasn't there," I said. "The fact is that he managed to stockpile it. You can draw an inference of negligence by the jailers if you want."

"I do," he said. "Indeed, I do, Mr. Rios. Not merely negligence, but gross negligence." He pushed his glasses back against his face from where they had slipped forward on his nose. Only his eyes reminded me of Jim. "As a proximate result of that gross negligence, I have been injured."

"You?" I asked.

He corrected himself. "My son has been directly injured," he said, "but certain interests of mine are also implicated."

Leaning forward, I said, "Mr. Pears, will you stop talking like a Supreme Court opinion and tell me what the hell it is you want from me?"

"I told you," he said, stiffening. "I intend to sue the county.

I want you to represent me or, rather, to represent Jim since the suit would be brought on his behalf."

I stared at him. "You son-of-a-bitch."

"Don't you dare address me in that manner."

"The night your son tried to kill himself you didn't even have the decency to show up at the hospital. I know that because I was there. And now you think I'm going to help you pick his bones?" I had leaned further across the table until I was within spitting distance of Pears. His face was aflame.

"We're not rich people," a tiny voice ventured from a corner of the room. I looked at Mrs. Pears. "Hospital care for Jim will be so expensive."

"Don't tell me you don't have medical insurance," I snapped. "Besides, if you had any respect for Jim you'd pull the plug and let him die."

"We're Catholics," she peeped.

"I was raised Catholic, Mrs. Pears," I said, "so I know all about Catholics like you who can't take a shit without consulting a priest."

Suddenly, Walter Pears jumped up, sending his chair skidding across the floor with a metallic shriek. I got up slowly until we faced each other.

Pears said, "If you were a man I'd kill you."

"If you were a man," I replied, "your son wouldn't be a goddamn vegetable in the jail ward of a charity hospital."

The door opened behind me. Judge Ryan's bailiff stuck his head into the room. "Everything okay here, folks?"

Mrs. Pears got to her feet. "Yes, officer. We were just leaving. Let's go, Walter." She tugged at his sleeve.

Pears seethed and stalked out of the room ahead of his wife. She stopped at the door and said to me, "There's a special place in hell for people like you."

After she left, the bailiff looked at me. "What was that all about?"

"Theology," I replied.

— 13 —

As I approached the door to Larry's house I heard the unmistakable noise of gunfire. I let myself in and called his name.

"In here," he shouted back.

I followed his voice to the study where I found him in his bathrobe, sitting on the sofa, watching a cassette on the TV. The cassette was frozen on the image of a man in a cop's uniform holding a gun.

"That sounded like the real thing."

"Stereo," Larry replied. He reached for a glass containing about a half-inch of brown fluid. Brandy. It disturbed me that he had taken up drinking again. He looked much the same as he had in October and insisted that his disease was still in remission. But he went into his office less and less often. My impression was that he now seldom left his house. It was even more difficult to talk to him about being sick, because he seemed to have reached a stage more of indifference than denial.

He had asked me to spend a few days with him. Since we were entering the holiday season and prosecutors were unwilling to face Christmas juries, it was a good time for me to get away.

"How did it go in court?" he asked.

I sat down beside him. "The charges were dismissed."

"Free at last," he muttered bitterly.

"When are you going to forgive Jim, Larry?"

He lifted his bony shoulders, dropped them and stared blankly at the frozen action on the screen.

"His parents asked me to sue the county," I said.

Larry made a disgusted noise. "Why?"

"For not preventing their little boy from trying to kill himself."

"Vultures," he said without heat.

"I thought so, too. Jim's dad and I got into a little scuffle."

"You draw blood?"

I shook my head.

"Too bad." He pushed a button on the remote control and the action on the screen began again.

"What are you watching?"

"Do you remember Sandy Blenheim?"

I nodded. "The agent."

"There's an actor he wants me to represent. Tom Zane. He's one of the stars of this show."

The cop on the screen raced down a dark alley in pursuit of a shadowy figure ahead of him. He commanded the figure to stop, then fired his gun. He came to the prone body, knelt and flipped it over. He saw the face of a boy and said, "Oh my God, Jerry."

"Who's the corpse?" I asked.

"The cop's son," Larry replied. "I've seen this one before."

On the screen the cop was sobbing. Then there was an aerial view of Los Angeles and the words "Smith & Wesson" appeared as music began playing. The screen split and displayed the faces of two men, one on each side. The man on the left was a white-haired, elegantly wrinkled old party who smiled benignly into the camera. On the right was one of the handsomest men I had ever seen. At first it was like looking at two different men. His slightly battered nose — it looked like it had been broken, then inexpertly set — and firmly moulded jaw gave his face a tough-ness that kept him from being a pretty boy. But there was pretti-ness, too, in the shape of his mouth, the long-lashed eyes. At second glance, though, the parts fit together with a kind of mas-culine elegance that reminded me of dim images from my child-hood of an earlier period of male stars, Tyrone Power or John Garfield. Only his dark hair seemed wrong, somehow.

Larry stopped the picture. "The fellow on the right is Zane."

"Who's the other?"

"Paul Houston. He's been on the tube for twenty years in

one series after another. This was supposed to be his show but Tom Zane's edged him out."

"Why? His looks?"

Larry sipped his brandy. "Watch."

He fast-forwarded the tape until he reached a scene in which Tom Zane was standing in the doorway of Paul Houston's office. Larry turned off the sound. Even with the sound off, Paul Houston was clearly an actor at work. His face was full of tics and pauses meant to convey, by turn, cranky good humor, concern, exasperation, and wisdom. It wasn't that his acting was obvious but merely that it was unmistakable. He was trying to reach the audience beyond the camera.

Tom Zane, on the other hand, hadn't the slightest interest in anything but the camera. He opened his face to it and the camera did all the work. It amounted to photography, not acting, and yet the effect was to intimate that, next to Tom Zane, Paul Houston looked like a wind-up toy. Larry shut off the tape and turned to me.

"See?" he said.

"He has a lot of charisma," I observed. "But can he act?"

Larry said, "He couldn't act his way out of the proverbial paper sack, but the camera loves his face."

"Well, it's some face. I've never heard of Tom Zane before."

"He came out of nowhere about a year ago and got a bit part in the pilot of this show. The response to him was so overwhelming that they killed off the actor who was originally supposed to play Houston's partner and replaced him with Zane."

"What's he want with you?"

"He's putting together a production company."

"I thought you weren't taking new business."

"Sandy's persistent," Larry said. "In fact, he was just here a while ago to drop off the cassette and," he picked up a paperback, "this."

I looked at the cover. "*Edward the Second* by Bertolt Brecht. Why?"

"Zane's performing the title role in a little theater on Santa Monica. Sandy wants me to come tonight."

"Are you?" I asked. We'd planned to have dinner out and take in a movie.

"If you'll come, too," he said, setting the book down.

"Sure," I said. "Did Sandy say anything about Jim Pears?"

Larry shook his head. "That was last week's sensation."

"Tough town you got here," I said. I picked up the book. "Isn't Brecht sort of ambitious for an actor who can't act?"

"I guess we'll find out tonight," Larry said. "It's kind of a vanity production."

"What does that mean?" I asked, flipping the pages of the play. It was in verse.

"Zane's producing it himself. It's not to make money but to show people in the industry what he can do as an actor. I suspect his wife's behind it."

"Who's that?"

"Irene Gentry."

"Irene Gentry?" I put the book down. "I saw her in *Long Day's Journey Into Night* three years ago. She's wonderful."

"Yeah," Larry said dubiously.

"What does that mean?"

"It's not about her acting. She really is a fine stage actress but in this town she has—" he smiled "— a reputation."

"What sort?"

"Nothing specific, just that she's difficult to work with. Not that she ever got much work here. She's always had too much going against her."

"For instance?"

"She's plain, she's now past forty, she's New York, and she's too damned good an actress."

"That's ridiculous."

"Which part?"

"All of it."

He lit a cigarette. "The days when movies could tolerate a Katherine Hepburn or Bette Davis as a leading lady are over. The public wants candy for the eyes. Irene Gentry is a five-course meal."

"I wrote her a fan letter once," I said.

"Henry, you surprise me."

I shrugged. "I was a lot younger, then," I offered, by way of explanation. "She was doing Shaw's *Caesar and Cleopatra*."

"Yes," Larry said, exhaling a stream of smoke, "I saw her in that, too."

We were both silent.

"Well, you may get to meet her tonight," he said, finishing his drink. "I'm going to take a nap, Henry. Wake me in an hour or so, all right?"

"All right." After he left I turned the tape back on, with the sound, and listened to Tom Zane deliver excruciatingly bad lines with all the animation of a robot. He was such a bad actor that it was almost possible to overlook his face. Almost. After a minute or two, I shut the tape off and picked up the Brecht.

☐

Edward the Second was an English king who ruled from 1307 to 1324. His calamitous reign culminated in a thirteen-year civil war that ended with his abdication. Two years later he was murdered by order of his wife's lover, a nobleman named Mortimer. Much of Edward's misfortune resulted from a love affair he conducted with a man named Piers Gaveston in an age when sodomy was a capital offense. Edward's homosexuality was less disturbing to his vassals than his insistence on carrying on openly with Gaveston. Parliament twice exiled Edward's lover only to have Edward recall him. Eventually, the nobility split between those who were loyal to the king and those who were repelled by him. This led to the civil war.

The notes in the Brecht book said that Edward's life had been the subject of an earlier play by Christopher Marlowe, the Elizabethan playwright who was himself homosexual. Marlowe's work was the source of much of Brecht's play. In Brecht's version, Edward — vain, frivolous, proud, willful, and incompetent — was more like the degenerate scion of the Krupp family than a fourteenth-century monarch. This characterization was emphasized by the way Brecht portrayed Gaveston, the object of Edward's passion. Gaveston was essentially a whore; a butcher's son who, for reasons inexplicable even to himself, was plucked from his low station by the whim of an infatuated king.

Gaveston was canny and fatalistic: the real hero of the Brecht play.

Though Edward was no hero he did have a certain grandeur which was mostly evident at the end of the play when he is held in captivity. In defeat and squalor, he repented nothing, becoming more of a king than when he actually governed.

The cost to Edward of his homosexuality was a gruesome death. While Brecht's stage directions indicated death by suffocation, the accompanying notes discussed the actual circumstances of Edward's murder. A red-hot poker was thrust into his anus. His last lover, who according to the historical record was not Gaveston, was castrated; his genitals were burned in public and then the man was decapitated.

□

The play was being performed in West Hollywood on Santa Monica Boulevard just east of La Cienega. Since I planned to see Josh Mandel after the play, Larry and I took separate cars. The rain had stopped at dusk and the skies had cleared. They were flooded with the lights of the city but, for all that, Santa Monica seemed dark and uninhabited as I waited at a traffic light just east of the Hollywood Memorial Cemetery.

Behind towering walls only the palm trees were visible. As I passed the gates I saw the domes and turrets of the necropolis. On the other side of the street, young boys — hustlers — stood in doorways or sat at bus stops watching cars with violent intensity. As I drove between the whores and the cemetery I thought of Jim Pears for whom death and sex had been in even closer proximity. When I came to Highland, brightly lit and busy, I felt like one awakening from the beginnings of a bad dream.

□

The theater was surprisingly small, a dozen rows of folding wooden chairs broken into three sections in a semi-circle ascending from the stage. Larry and I sat third row center, arriving just as the lights began to dim. There were few other people around us. One of them was a woman with a familiar face. She glanced at me and then turned away.

"That's Irene Gentry," I said, more to myself than to Larry.

He looked over at her and nodded.

The house lights went out around us and I looked at the stage. A remarkably handsome man stood in the lights holding a piece of paper — it was Edward's lover, Gaveston. He lifted it toward his eyes and said:

> My father, old Edward, is dead. Come quickly
> Gaveston, and share the kingdom with your
> dearest friend, King Edward the Second.

There followed a scene in which Gaveston was approached by two itinerant soldiers who offered him their service. He mockingly refused and one of them cursed him to die at the hands of a soldier. The three of them then stepped into the shadows. Five other men emerged. One was Edward.

"Where's Zane?" I whispered to Larry.

"The blond."

I looked. "His hair—" I began, remembering that on the TV show he had had black hair.

"This is natural color," Larry said. "They made him dye it for the series because Houston is also blond. Or was, rather, twenty years ago."

"He's short," I said. Zane looked no taller than five-seven.

"He wears lifts in front of the camera," Larry explained. He looked at me and smiled. "Poor Henry, this must be terribly disillusioning."

Someone shushed us and I returned my attention to the stage. Beneath the glare of the stage lights, Zane's face lost the magic that the camera conjured up. He was still handsome but his face was oddly immobile; I diagnosed a case of the jitters. He delivered his first line, "I will have Gaveston," as if requesting his coffee black.

Midway through the play two things were apparent. First, as Larry had warned me, Tom Zane could not act. Second, the cast that surrounded him had been carefully directed to disguise Zane's disability as much as humanly possible. All except Gaveston. I glanced at my program. The actor playing Gaveston was named Antony Good. While the other actors covered Zane's fluffed lines, Good stared at Zane in open amazement as he raced through yet another speech, spitting it out like sour milk. The other actors underacted assiduously when playing a scene with Zane, but Good threw himself into the role of Gaveston in open competition with the star. It was a one-sided contest. Good was superb, bringing to the character of Gaveston the pathos of the street outside the theater.

Zane, by contrast, lumbered through these scenes like a wounded animal dragging itself to a burial ground. Sweat soaked his underarms and he sprayed spittle across the stage. Once or twice he simply stopped mid-speech and gasped for air. Then, frowning with concentration, he would begin again, devastating Brecht's elegant lines. I looked around to Irene Gentry. She sat, motionless, eyes facing the stage.

When the house lights went on at intermission, she was already gone.

Larry looked at me and said, almost irritably, "Whatever possessed him to do this play?"

"It is terrible, isn't it?"

"No," Larry replied. "He's terrible."

We got up to stretch.

"Gaveston is excellent, though," I said.

"Mm. It's a role Tony Good's played in his life."

"You know him?"

"Oh, yes," he said in a curious voice.

"Meaning?"

"Tony sometimes offers his services as an escort to men of a certain age."

"Have you ever taken him up on it?"

Larry shook his head. "No. I'm going outside to get some air. You coming?"

We went out.

□

In the first scene of the second half of the play Gaveston was killed. Tom Zane's performance began to improve at once. In the final scenes, where Edward is dragged from castle to castle alone except for his jailers, Zane was transformed. His delivery was still awkward but the suffering he conveyed was authentic. Not just Zane's expressions, but the contours of his face and his body changed so that he seemed a different man from the one who first stepped upon the stage. I began to believe that he was Edward the Second.

The culmination of his performance came in the assassination sequence. In the play, Edward has been locked in a cell in London, into which the city's sewage drops upon him. Drums are pounded to keep him from sleeping. The assassin, Lightborn, is let into Edward's cell.

The scene began in darkness. Slowly, a blue light glimmered from a corner of the stage where a man stood, arms loose at his sides, face tilted upward toward the light. His hair was matted and his body covered with filth. This was Zane. In the flickering blue light it took me a moment to see that, other than a soiled rag that cupped his genitals, he was naked. Zane had a first-class body. He said:

> This hole they've put me in is a cesspit.
> For seven hours the dung of London
> Has dropped on me.

A ladder of rope dropped from above the stage and an immense, powerfully muscled black man climbed down. Lightborn. At once, Zane accused him of being his murderer. Lightborn denied it.

Zane answered, "Your look says death and nothing else."

The drums that had been heard from the beginning of the scene were suddenly still. Lightborn went to a brazier where he lit a coal fire. Zane watched impassively. An amber light was added to the stage. Then, approaching the king as he would a lover, Lightborn coaxed him to lie down on his cot and sleep. Zane resisted.

Pulling away, Zane turned to face Lightborn and again accused him of being sent as his murderer.

Lightborn touched his fingers to Zane's filthy hair, picked out a bit of straw and repeated, "You have not slept. You're tired, Sire. Lie down on the bed and rest a while."

Zane turned to face the audience. Lightborn quietly approached him from behind and lifted his powerful arms which he wrapped around Zane's chest as if intending to squeeze the

life from him. Zane did not resist. Lightborn released his arms
and once again urged the king to sleep.

Zane replied:

> The rain was good. Not eating made me full. But
> The darkness was the best. . . .
> Therefore let
> The dark be dark and the unclean unclean.
> Praise hunger, praise mistreatment, praise
> The darkness.

Lightborn led Zane by the hand to a cot and Zane lay down.
Looking at Lightborn he said, "There's something buzzing in my
ears. It whispers: If I sleep now, I'll never wake. It's anticipation
that makes me tremble so." He delivered these lines softly, as if
speaking in a dream. I thought of Jim Pears. I glanced at Larry
and wondered what he was thinking.

Lightborn kissed Zane on the lips. Then there was silence.
Zane's breath grew light and rapid as he slipped into sleep. The
cot creaked as he turned on his stomach. Lightborn raised his
hand into the air and caught a metal poker tossed down from
where the ladder had come. He placed the tip of the poker in the
brazier. The blue light flickered out, leaving only the amber
which slowly changed to deep red.

Lightborn stood above Zane holding the poker a foot or two
above Zane and aimed it directly between his legs, upward
toward his anus. He flexed his powerful arms. The light went
out.

Zane's shriek rent the darkness.

It was only then that I remembered that the poker scene
was not in Brecht's play.

— 14 —

The actors took their bows and filed off the stage. Larry and I got up and made our way to the aisle. Sandy Blenheim, wearing pleated black leather pants and a voluminous white shirt, stopped us. He grabbed Larry's hand and said, "You made it."

"Hello, Sandy," Larry replied, disengaging his hand. "You remember Henry Rios."

"Hello," I said.

Blenheim took me in with a reptilian flick of his eyes.

"You were that kid's lawyer," he said. "Too bad about him. It would have been a great movie." To Larry he said, "Wasn't T. Z. fabulous?"

"He got better toward the end," Larry replied.

"The last scene," Blenheim went on. "Perfect. You know it was his idea to do it with just the jock strap."

"That last scene wasn't in Brecht," I said. "Brecht has Lightborn suffocate Edward."

"T. Z., again," Blenheim replied. "Someone told him that's how the guy really died, so he wanted to do it that way." He looked at me. "It's kinda sexy, huh?"

"Yes," I allowed. "It was."

Blenheim smiled again as if confirming something about me. I could imagine what it was. I knew a tribesman when I saw one. So, it seemed, did he. He wagged a finger between Larry and me. "You two dating?"

Larry cut him off. "We're friends, Sandy."

"Well, why don't you and your friend come over to Monet's. Tom and Rennie are having a little party."

'Henry?"

"Sure," I replied, thinking that I might meet Irene Gentry there.

"That's great," Blenheim said. "Maybe you and me and Tom can get together about that contract, Larry."

"Okay," Larry replied without enthusiasm.

"See you there," Blenheim said. He favored me with another narrow smile, and bounced off shouting the name of his next victim.

"Who's Rennie?" I asked.

"Irene Gentry. The name Irene doesn't really lend itself to abbreviation, but everyone calls her Rennie."

"Rennie," I repeated.

"Let's go meet her."

□

The sky was clear but starless. Only a trickle of water in the gutters gave any clue of the day's rain. Santa Monica Boulevard was clogged with traffic — brake lights flared in the darkness, wheels squeaked to a halt — and the air was choked with exhaust fumes. Larry cadged a cigarette from a passerby and lit it.

"Monet's isn't far," he said. "Let's walk it."

It was Friday night and the bars were doing brisk business. Country-western music blared from one in which, through smoked windows, male couples did the Texas two-step. Outside another bar a gaggle of street kids offered us coke. At a fast food shack, painted bright orange and lit up like a birthday cake, Larry stopped to buy a pack of cigarettes. A boy with stringy hair downed the house specialty, a pastrami burrito. I found the phone and called Josh Mandel. He answered on the second ring.

I explained that I was going to a party. "If you still want to get together," I added, "I could meet you in about an hour." I wanted him to say yes.

"Okay," he said. "That's fine."

"Your place?"

"Where are you now?" he asked.

I stuck my head out of the booth and looked in vain for a street sign. "On Santa Monica," I replied. "There's a Mayfair market across the street."

After a moment's pause he said, "Oh, King's Road. There's a bar just east of Fairfax called the Hawk. South side of the boulevard. I could meet you there."

"All right. In about an hour."

"Mr. Rios?" he began, awkwardly.

"Yes, Josh?"

"It's a gay bar."

Larry came up and tapped on the phone booth.

"I've got to go now," I said. "I'll see you then."

I hung the phone up and stepped out of the booth.

"Josh Mandel is gay," I told Larry as we resumed walking down the street.

"The guy who testified against Jim?"

"The star witness," I replied.

□

Monet's was a squat windowless building painted charcoal gray next to a porn shop. Marble steps led up from the filthy sidewalk to double wooden doors presided over by a man in a red jacket. He opened the door for us. Inside, at a plexiglass lectern, stood another red jacket. A huge Motherwell hung on the wall behind him. Two halls led off from the small foyer. The familiar sounds of a restaurant were absent. Instead, expensive silence reigned.

"Gentlemen?" the red jacket inquired.

"Zane party," Larry said.

"Very good," he said, just like in the movies, and summoned a third red jacket. "The Morgan Room."

We were led down one of the halls. In the coppery light I saw that the walls were marble.

"What is this place?" I asked Larry.

"A membership restaurant," he replied, lighting a cigarette and flicking the match to the carpeted floor. "You come in and you're assigned a private dining room."

"Is the point privacy?"

"No," Larry said. "The point is status."

We came to a door. The red jacket opened it and stepped aside to let us pass. The room looked like the conference room of a particularly stodgy law firm; all dark paneling and copper fixtures, Winslow Homer paintings on the walls and even brass spittoons. There were a lot of people inside, including some of the cast members, milling around with the provisional air of people waiting for a party to begin.

"This is going to be business for me," Larry said. "You mind being on your own?"

"No. I'm leaving in about an hour anyway."

"Come and find me on your way out."

I went over to one of two tables set with food. A dark-haired waiter asked me what I'd like. All that the various dishes had in common was that they were fashionable. There was sushi, crepes, antipasto, pasta salads, rolled sandwiches in pita bread, crudites, ham and smoked turkey, cheeses, and breads. I ate a bit of sushi. It wasn't fresh.

Beside me a woman said, "Stick to the raw vegetables."

I looked around. "Hello," I said.

The woman who had spoken to me smiled. She had a round, pretty face. Her dark hair was streaked with two colors, burgundy and red. She was not, perhaps, as young as she looked.

"You were in the play," I said. "You played Edward's wife."

"You came in with Larry Ross," she replied, helping herself to a radish.

"You know him?"

"Only by reputation. He's out of my league. Are you a lawyer, too?"

"Yes, but not that kind."

"Expensive?" She bit into the radish with preternaturally white teeth.

"No, entertainment. I practice criminal defense."

She drew in her cheeks a bit. "Who's in trouble?"

"I'm not here on business," I replied.

"Don't be absurd. Everyone here's on business. My name is Sarah."

"Henry," I replied. "You were very good as Anne."

"I hope you're a better lawyer than a critic," she said, examining a piece of cauliflower. Suddenly there was applause around the door. The Zanes entered with Sandy Blenheim hard on their heels. As they swept past me, Irene Gentry and I caught each other's eyes. She seemed to smile.

"The Macbeths," Sarah said, dryly. She dropped the unfinished radish back on the tray and joined the Zanes' entourage.

I turned my attention to Irene Gentry. In a black cocktail dress she moved across the room like an exclamation mark. Her long hair was swept over a bare shoulder. There were diamonds at her neck. Blenheim directed her and Tom Zane to a little group dominated by a white-haired man in a tweed jacket who was making a big show of lighting a meerschaum pipe. I moved closer to watch her. She laid a hand lightly on the man's wrist as he spoke and his shoulders seemed to inflate. Her husband, meanwhile, had backed himself against the wall with a pretty girl. Blenheim watched them for a moment, then broke them up and brought Zane back into the group.

I was standing behind the man to whom Irene Gentry was speaking. She looked past his shoulder at me. Our eyes met and her face formed a question. A moment later she excused herself and came over.

"I know you, don't I?" she asked in her famous voice.

"I wish I could say you did, Miss Gentry."

"My friends call me Rennie." She gazed at me intently and without embarrassment.

"Weren't you the lawyer for Jim Pears?" she asked.

"Yes. Henry Rios. How did you know that?"

She smiled. "Sandy was very interested in buying the rights to the story as a property for Tom. Didn't he approach you?"

"Yes," I replied, "but he didn't say who he was working for."

"Tom's his biggest client," she said, absently.

"Well," I replied, "I don't know anything about acting but your husband seems a bit old to play Jim Pears."

She seemed puzzled for a moment, then laughed. "I think the idea was for Tom to play you."

"Me?"

"The boy's lawyer," she replied. "Of course, we didn't know it was going to be you until we saw it on the news." She glanced around the room. "It's odd to find you here."

I explained that I had come with Larry Ross.

"Oh, Larry," she said. "He's our—" She looked at me, as if

for help. "Who was the Greek who carried the lamp looking for an honest man?"

"Diogenes," I replied, guessing that she'd known that all along.

She said, "I'm not making fun of him, Henry. I admire him. More now than ever."

I felt the heat rising to my face from my neck. "I don't understand."

She looked at me, tenderly. "Of course I know he's ill," she said. "We all know." Her glance swept across the room.

"He doesn't know that."

She laid her hand across my wrist. "He won't find out from me."

"Thank you."

"Did you enjoy the play?" she asked, dropping her hand, her voice light.

"Toward the end, especially."

"Not because you thought it was ending, I hope." She moved a bit closer. She smelled of roses.

"Your husband seemed to get his bearings in the second half."

"Tom's not a stage actor," she replied. "But on the whole I don't think he did too bad a job of it."

"You would have been perfect to play Anne."

Her smile was charming and wise. "Discretion is often the better part of marriage."

Her skin glistened, faintly, as if moistened by dew. I felt an overwhelming desire to touch her. I took her hand. "Do you mind?"

"Of course not," she replied, but then I suppose she was used to men wanting to touch her. "Tell me about Jim Pears. What will happen to him now?"

"The charges against him were dismissed," I said. "He'll never regain consciousness. Eventually, he'll die."

She studied me silently, then said, "You have the face of a man who feels too much."

As there was nothing to say to this, I said nothing.

She tugged at my hand. "Come and meet Tom."

Tom Zane stepped forward from the people he had been talking to and said to his wife, "You're trying to make me jealous."

This close, he looked to be in his mid-thirties. Small lines puckered the edges of his eyes and lips. His skin, still tanned, was faintly freckled. Clusters of broken veins had begun to surface around the edges of his nostrils, the sure sign of a drinker. He gave off the scent of an expensive cologne. His eyes were a deep, serene blue. Though he cast a blond's golden glow it was diluted by his hard, false cheerfulness.

Irene said, "Tom, this is Henry Rios. Jim Pears's lawyer."

Zane looked at me blankly for a moment, then said, "Oh, the gay kid. Sandy talked to you."

"Briefly."

Zane smiled. "You're too good-looking to be a lawyer. You look more like a wetback gigolo."

"I was at the play," I said, ignoring the comment. "Your last scenes were very moving."

"Or maybe a diplomat. Come on, Rennie," he said, and took her from me.

"Join us, Henry," she said, as her hand slipped from my fingers.

A circle of well-wishers formed around us and I stood at the edge of conversation as the Zanes received them. Irene — Rennie — handled them as skillfully as a politician and it appeared that she truly did not forget faces. Or names, or names of spouses, children, or dogs. She told funny stories on herself and listened to less funny stories which she made comic by her superbly timed reactions. Now and then, she'd lift her eyes and smile at me as if we shared a secret.

Tom Zane, on the other hand, seemed talented only at being admired. When he wasn't being praised he looked off with a vague smile to the other side of the room. He drank three glasses of champagne and was about to take a fourth when Sandy Blenheim intercepted it. Tom surrendered the glass with a shrug. He nibbled at a plate of food that Blenheim brought him. He seemed both bored and bewildered. I excused myself to look for Larry.

"Don't leave without saying goodbye," Rennie said.

"I won't."

Larry was talking to Tony Good, the actor who had played Gaveston. Tony Good was drunk. I complimented him on his performance.

"It's not easy playing against T. Z.," he said. "He's lousy. Who are you anyway?"

"Henry Rios," I said.

"Oh, yeah. Another gay lawyer? You're kinda cute, Henry. You gotta lover?" He reached for a glass of champagne from a passing waiter and tipped the tray, spilling the drinks on himself. The room was momentarily still.

"Shit," he said. A red jacket rushed over with a napkin and tried to dry Good's shirt. "Never mind the shirt," he said. "How about another drink."

Larry said, "You're drunk enough, Tony." To me he said, "I'm going to drive him home."

"Fine."

"Come on, Tony," Larry said. "It's time to go."

Tony Good smiled. "Will you tuck me in?"

"Not if you're still charging by the hour," Larry replied.

"Bitch," Tony said. To me he said, "You come, too. We'll make it a threesome."

"Another time," I said.

"Lemme give you my number," Tony said.

"I'm sure Larry has it," I said.

"No," Tony said. "Just take a minute." He scribbled a number on the back of a card that he fished out of his pocket and shoved it at me.

"Thanks," I said, accepting it.

"Call me," he shouted as Larry hustled him out the door.

Remembering the hangovers I got from champagne, I felt very sorry for Tony Good. I checked my watch; I had already overstayed the hour I had allowed myself. I looked around for Rennie to say goodbye, but neither she nor Zane were in the room. Sandy Blenheim was standing at the bar talking to the bartender. I approached them.

"Hello, Sandy," I said.

He glanced at me with annoyance. The bartender looked relieved and slipped away.

"Hi," he said. "Enjoying yourself?"

"The party's fine but I've got to go. I wondered if you'd say goodbye to Miss Gentry for me."

"Yeah, I saw you talking with her," he said. "You two know each other?"

"Not before tonight."

He picked up a tall glass from the bar and drank. When he set it down he wiped his mouth with the back of his hand. "What did you talk about?"

"This and that," I replied, disliking him.

"Yeah," he said. "You're gay, right?"

"I don't make a secret about it."

"Just making sure," he said. "Tom's the jealous kind."

Having seen Zane in action earlier with another woman, I doubted this, but said, "He has nothing to worry about from me."

"So," Sandy said, lowering his voice, "what are you doing later?"

I smiled. "I've got a date."

"And after that?"

"Just say goodbye to Rennie for me," I said.

"Sure," he replied, already losing interest. His glance drifted back to the bartender. "Hey, Nick, another drink."

On my way out I stopped at the men's room. As I stood at the urinal I heard the door open. When I went to wash my hands I found Tom Zane stooped over the marble counter that held the wash basins. He lifted his eyes to the mirror and saw me.

"It's the ambassador," he said. He inhaled a line of coke, straightened up, tilted his head back and sniffled. "Want some?"

"No thanks." I turned on the tap and ran my hands beneath the water. He did another line.

"Is that safe to do here?" I asked.

"Are you gonna tell?"

"No."

"Good." He did a third line and stood up, putting his arm

arouna my shoulder. "As long as you're not one of Sandy's spies."

"I'm not."

"He says you're gay. Is that right?"

"Yeah," I replied.

Zane dropped his arm to just above my waist and we looked at each other in the mirror. In the dim light he looked almost as he had in the last scene of the play: heroic, dissipated, and beautiful.

"We should get together sometime," he said.

Before I could think of an answer to this, the door opened again. He dropped his arm to his side and stepped away. I dried my hands. Sandy Blenheim came in, looked at us and scowled.

"Listen, T. Z., there's some important people out there wanting to meet you."

"Don't I get to take a leak?"

"What's he do," Blenheim said, pointing at me, "hold your dick?"

I said, "Looks to me like that's your job, Sandy."

"That's telling him, Ambassador."

"Come on, T. Z., you're wasting time." Blenheim grabbed Zane's arm and dragged him out.

I watched them go, then finished drying my hands. I looked at myself in the mirror. Zane's proposition hadn't meant anything more than Tony Good's or Sandy Blenheim's had. They were empty gestures, the kind it was beginning to seem that these people were full of. As I adjusted the knot in my tie, I tried to imagine Tom Zane as me, and burst out laughing.

— 15 —

The Hawk occupied a space in a row of stores between a deli and a manicurist. A blue awning over the entrance was the bar's only distinguishing feature. I parked on the street and made my way over to the bar. A couple of men in 501s and flannel shirts were standing at the entrance drinking from bottles of Budweiser. I was wearing a gray suit, a maroon tie, and wingtips. We exchanged friendly nods as I pushed through the upholstered door.

The front room was a long, narrow rectangle with the bar running the length of it. Opposite the bar, stacks of beer boxes were pushed up against the wall. The room was packed and there was only a small aisle between the men lined up against the bar and those leaning against the beer boxes. The place smelled of spilt beer and cigarettes and was lit in red by spotlights above the bar. Dolly Parton was belting out a song from the overhead speakers and everywhere mouths moved, singing along with her. I wedged my way down the room looking for Josh Mandel.

There was a pool room behind the bar. A green-shaded light hung over the pool table. A thin boy with a bad complexion waited while his opponent, a lumbering bear of a man, calculated a shot. Josh Mandel was sitting on a bar stool beneath a chalkboard that listed the order of players. He wore jeans and an old white button-down shirt and his glasses dangled out of his pocket. A red sweater was spread across his knees. He was smoking a cigarette with one hand while the other grasped a bottle of beer. He looked too young to be either smoking or drinking. I came around the room until I was standing beside him.

"Josh?"

He jerked his face toward me. "Mr. Rios."

"Henry," I replied. "I'm sorry I'm late."

"That's okay." He smiled at me. "You want a drink?"

"I don't drink. Is there somewhere quiet we can talk?"

"There's a patio out back," he said, and hopped off the bar stool. "Come on."

He led me out to a small fenced-in courtyard in the center of which was a big firepit. It was dark except for a couple of lights above the exit and the glow of the fire. We sat down on a bench beneath the feathery leaves of a jacaranda tree. Josh put on his glasses and the red sweater.

"I guess you figured out I'm gay," he said.

"I assume that's why you told me to meet you here."

He nodded. "You knew when you saw me in court the first time."

I remembered the odd jolt of recognition I'd felt that day when I had looked at him. I said, "I'm not sure. Maybe."

He finished his beer. A waiter came by and Josh asked for a screwdriver. I asked for mineral water.

"Did Jim know about you?" I asked.

"No one does," he said. "You probably think I should be more out."

"That's not my business."

"I just mean, you're out and everything."

"I learned pretty early on that I'm not a good liar. That's all there is to my being out."

He lowered his eyes. "It's not like I like lying," he said, softly.

"I didn't mean it that way."

"You don't have to like me, Henry," he said, suddenly. Our eyes met and I felt his sadness. Or maybe I felt my own. "You didn't come to talk about me, anyway. You want to know about Jim."

The waiter brought our drinks. I paid for them over Josh's protests. "What about him?"

He churned his drink with a straw. "It's something I found out after he tried to kill himself. I was hanging around the bar at the Yellowtail one night and the bartender asked me to dump the trash. He gave me the bar key to the back door. It was new."

"New?" I echoed.

"Uh-huh. I asked him what happened to the old one and he said it had disappeared months ago. The next day I went through work orders and stuff and I found this." He pulled his wallet out of his back pocket and extracted a piece of paper, handing it to me.

I examined it. It was a receipt from a locksmith for the making of a key. The receipt was dated less than a week after the night Brian Fox was murdered. I handed it back to Josh.

"You think the missing key has something to do with Brian's death?"

He folded the paper. "You'd need it to get out," he said.

I thought about this. "You think there was someone back there before Brian came in?"

He nodded.

"Kind of a strange coincidence," I said.

"There's a strongbox down in the manager's office," Josh said. "Someone could've cleaned it out and let himself out through the back door."

"A burglary?" I was interested, suddenly, in the missing key. "And Brian just happened to be there. Had the strongbox been tampered with?"

Josh shook his head. "That doesn't mean they didn't try." He shivered and pulled a pack of cigarettes from his shirt pocket. The fire cast a flickering light on his face.

"The problem is that they found Jim with the knife," I said. "There doesn't seem to be any way around that."

"Oh, that's right," he said too quickly and gulped his drink.

I looked at him. He hadn't asked me here to tell me about the key. Then why? To let me know about himself?

"Still," I said, "I'll have my investigator look into it."

"That skinny black guy?"

"Yes. Freeman Vidor. He talked to you, didn't he?"

Josh frowned. "Yeah. I'm going to get another drink. You want one?"

"No." He got up and started for the bar. "Josh," I said, "are you trying to get drunk?"

He sat down again and looked at me. "I could've told you about the key on the phone," he said, then added awkwardly, "I just really wanted to see you again."

I looked at him. "Why?"

"I've seen you before," he said.

"I beg your pardon?"

"Two years ago you gave a speech at a rally at UCLA against the sodomy law. Remember?"

"I gave so many speeches that year," I said apologetically.

He smiled. "I remember. Afterwards I came up and shook your hand." The smile faded and he looked at me gravely. "You gave me the courage to be who I am. But it didn't last."

"Few of us come out all at once," I said, gently. "It's not the easiest thing to do."

He shook his head and frowned. "I never came out at all."

"We are at a gay bar," I said.

"It's easy to come out in a bar," he said, "or in bed." A shadow crossed his face.

"Are you all right?"

He stared down at his hands and said, "No."

There was a lot of pain in the little word. He grabbed my hand, clutching it tightly.

"What is it, Josh?" I asked.

He drew a shaky breath. "My life's a lie," he said. "No one knows who I really am, not my friends or my folks. I can't live this way anymore."

Suddenly I thought of Jim Pears. "Don't say that," I said sharply.

He let go of my hand and looked away from me.

"I'm sorry," he said in a voice at the edge of tears. "I admire you so much. I wanted you to like me."

"I didn't mean to snap at you. It's just when you said you couldn't live this way, it made me think of Jim."

"If it wasn't for me, he would be all right," Josh said.

"You're taking the blame for a lot," I replied.

"If I'd told him I was gay—" he began.

"It wouldn't have made any difference," I said. "His denial was too deep."

Josh tipped his head back against the fence. The light from the doorway of the bar shone on his face and cast a sort of halo around his hair.

"Is that true?" he asked.

"Yes."

He inclined his face toward me. "But you still don't like me."

"You lied to me about where you were the night Brian was killed."

Someone dropped a glass and it shattered near the firepit.

"I wasn't anywhere near the restaurant," he said.

"But you didn't tell me the truth."

He rose from the bench and stood irresolutely. "I told you," he said, looking toward the bar. "My life's a lie."

He made a move to go.

"Wait," I said.

His look was disbelieving. "You want me to stay?"

"You asked me here to come out to me," I said. "That couldn't have been easy. I did a lot of harm to Jim by not listening to him. I don't want to make the same mistake with you."

He sat down.

"So," I continued, "you want to talk?"

He shook his head. "No, I want you to come home with me."

I smiled. "You need a friend, Josh, not another trick."

"It doesn't have to mean anything to you to mean something to me."

"That's not the point."

He touched my hand. "Are we really going to sit here and talk about this?

I looked up at him, saw my face reflected in his glasses and saw past my reflection into his eyes. A waiter came up and asked us if we wanted another drink.

"No," I said. "We're leaving."

□

Josh lived in Hollywood on a decayed street lined alternately with boxy apartment buildings and little stucco houses whose front yards doubled as driveways. The squalor was softened by the big elm trees that lined the road and the wild rose bushes still putting forth their flowers four weeks before Christmas. I lowered my window as I followed his car down the street. Mariachi music blared from one of the houses where four men squatted on the front lawn guzzling beer. Lights were on in every house, though it was now near two in the morning.

Josh flicked his signal and turned into the carport of a two-storey apartment building. I pulled up along the curb and got out of my car. He met me at the sidewalk. It was cold. Behind us, in the Hollywood Hills, the lights flickered like distant stars. The big emptiness of the night was like a stage as we stood in the grainy light of a streetlamp looking at each other. In the darkness, I smelled jasmine.

"This is it," he said, nervously.

I put my arm around his shoulders, and felt the tension in his neck seep out as he leaned into me.

"You're cold," I observed, touching his face with the back of my hand.

"Let's go upstairs."

He led me around to a tall gate, through it, and up a concrete staircase to the second floor landing. "The place is kind of a mess," he said, unlocking the door.

He held the door open for me. The room I found myself in was, in fact, quite tidy. There was a fake Oriental rug on a fake parquet floor. A shabby couch flanked by two sling armchairs, and a glass-topped coffee table furnished the place. One wall was taken up by wooden bookshelves crammed with books. A stereo and a small TV were set on a couple of orange crates filled with records.

Josh stood beside me. "Can I get you something to drink?"

"No, thank you."

"Excuse me, then," he said, and went into a small kitchen.

The far wall was curtained. I went over and lifted the curtains, revealing a small patio behind a sliding glass door. I sat down on the couch. There was a fish bowl filled with change on the coffee table and next to it a photograph in a heavy bronze frame. The photograph showed a handsome middle-aged couple, two pretty girls, and a smiling Josh. He came back into the room holding a glass of milk.

"Your family?"

He nodded and sat down beside me. "My dad's a CPA," he said.

"Where do they live?"

"Sherman Oaks." He set the glass down on the table. "Are you comfortable?"

I loosened my tie.

Smiling faintly, Josh asked, "Is that as relaxed as you get?"

"It's been a long time."

"For me, too," he said. "I don't want you to think I spend all my time at bars or anything."

"I know."

"This feels like the first time for me," he said, then smiled nervously. "That's the wrong thing to say, isn't it?"

I held him. "No," I said. "My first time was almost twenty years ago. We thought we had invented love."

He kissed me. His mouth tasted of milk and his skin beneath my fingers was smooth and firm. He drew back and unknotted my tie, sliding it from my collar, and unbuttoned my shirt. I removed my jacket and tossed it aside. Sinking into the couch, I pulled him against me.

"What happened to him?" Josh asked.

"To whom?"

"Your first time."

"She got married."

He lifted his head and looked at me. "It was a girl?"

"Yes," I replied.

"Were you gay?"

"I've always been gay, Josh. I just happened to be in love with a girl." I kicked off my shoes and smiled at him. "You can't always specialize."

His dark eyes were unhappy. "Do you still go out with them?"

"Women? No," I said. "She was the only one."

He smiled. "That cuts down the competition."

"Don't worry about that. It's a buyer's market."

"We'll see," he said with a lewd flicker in his eyes.

Some time later we lay on the couch, facing each other, our clothes discarded, bodies touching.

I watched my face form in Josh's eyes. "You called me the night Jim tried to kill himself," I said.

He was surprised. "How did you know it was me?"

"Just a feeling. I wish you hadn't hung up."

"I lost my nerve," he replied and smiled. "Are you tired?"

I pressed him against me. "In a minute."

□

It was cold. I opened my eyes and found that Josh had rolled himself into the blankets and now slept contentedly at the edge of the narrow bed. A light shone from beneath the bathroom door. He had carefully arranged my suit on a chair, leaving his own clothes in a little pile beside it. I gently unwound the blankets from him and lay against his back, putting my arm across his chest. He smelled of sweat and soap and semen. I lowered my hand to his firm belly, cupped his genitals and laid my hand, finally, between his thighs. He moved his head a fraction and I knew he was awake. He pressed his rump against my groin. I raised my hand along his torso to his nipples and grazed them with my palm. He sighed and pushed harder.

"Do you want to?" he whispered.

I raised myself on my elbow and said, "Of course I do, but I haven't carried rubbers with me since I was sixteen."

"Just this once," he said. "You could pull out before — you know."

I squeezed his neck between my fingers. "No," I said softly. "There's AIDS, Josh. It's not worth the risk."

Abruptly he drew away to the edge of the bed and lay on his back, looking at the darkness.

"I didn't mean that the way it sounded," I said.

"I know what you meant," he said in a flat voice. "You're right. It's not worth it."

He drew himself rigidly apart from me as if daring me to make a move across the channel of darkness between us.

"That's not what I meant at all," I said, reaching for him.

He jerked away. "I said it didn't have to mean anything to you, Henry."

I lay back in the bed. "You've been awfully rough on yourself tonight, Josh. I'd like to know why."

"Does it really matter to you?" he asked, more in pain than defiance.

But I had long ago stopped issuing blank checks on my emotions and I waited a moment too long to answer.

"That's what I thought," he said.

"What's this about, Josh?"

Instead of answering, he turned away and quietly began to weep.

— 16 —

When he stopped crying, I asked, "Does this have anything to do with Jim?"

"Please hold me," Josh said. I moved myself against him and took him in my arms, feeling the dull thud of his heart against my ribs. "I don't want to talk now."

I opened my mouth to speak but thought better of it. After a few minutes, Josh slipped into sleep. A long time later, I did, too.

When I woke Josh was standing beside me, dressed in jeans and a UCLA sweatshirt. He squinted at me through his glasses. It was plain that he was seeing a stranger.

"I'll make you some breakfast," he said, politely.

"Coffee will be fine."

He nodded and left. I stretched my neck, shaking off the little aches that seemed to accumulate there as I got older, wiping the sleep from my eyes. The bathroom was steamy and smelled of Josh. A thin, suspicious face formed in the mirror. Deepening lines and graying hair foretold the coming of middle-age, what the French called — ironically, in my case — the age of discretion. I rinsed my mouth, showered, put on the clothes I had worn the night before, and followed the smell of coffee into the kitchen.

Josh stood at the stove scrambling eggs. He looked at me and said, "You should eat something."

"Whatever you're having." I poured coffee into a mug from Disneyland and leaned against the counter, watching him.

"Do you ever stop thinking?" he asked.

"I did last night," I replied. He stirred the eggs savagely.

"Lowered your standards, you mean."

"That's not what I mean."

"Don't worry about it." He shut off the flame beneath the skillet and faced me.

"What were you going to tell me last night?"

"Nothing."

I set my cup on the counter. "We shouldn't start out by lying to each other."

He jammed his hands into his pockets. "Sometimes I don't think there is any love, just a kind of envy." He looked at me. "I want to be who you are. What do you want from me, to be twenty-two again?"

"I think I'd better be on my way," I said.

He started to say something but then simply nodded. I let myself out. I told myself I didn't want to buy into his troubles, but I felt heavier going down the steps than I had coming up.

□

There was a black Mercedes parked in front of Larry's house. The plate read GLDNBOY. I pulled into the driveway and went into the house. Tom Zane, Irene Gentry, and Sandy Blenheim were sitting in the big front room with Larry. The coffee table was littered with papers, coffee cups, and empty glasses. A half-empty bottle of Old Bushmill's sat near an ashtray filled with cigarette butts.

"Excuse me," I said.

Larry gave me a look that made me acutely aware that I was in the same clothes I had worn the night before. "I think you know everyone," he said.

"Looks like someone got lucky last night," Zane said.

"I don't mean to interrupt," I said, and headed up the stairs without looking back. I changed clothes and called Freeman Vidor. He was surprised to hear from me.

"Read about you in the paper today," he said. "D.A. dumped the Pears case."

"Justice triumphs again," I replied. Downstairs someone burst into loud laughter.

"You don't sound like a happy man."

From the window I watched shadows of clouds gather on the surface of Silver Lake. "It wasn't exactly an acquittal."

"He wasn't exactly innocent."

"There's something I'd like you to look into."

"We still talking about Pears?"

"Yes."

"I don't do *pro bono*," he said.

"I'll pay you the same rate we originally agreed on."

"Go ahead."

I told him about the missing bar key.

"That's it?" His voice was incredulous. "You think someone broke in, slashed the Fox kid and left the knife in Pears's hand?"

"I'm less interested in the bar key than I am in Josh Mandel," I replied after a moment's hesitation.

"What does that mean?"

"I think he's concealing information about the case," I replied. "I'd like you to find out what it is without approaching him."

"I'm an investigator, Henry, not a psychic."

There was more laughter from downstairs. "Then do what you have to do," I replied.

"What do you think he knows?"

"I have no idea," I said, irritably. "That's what I'm hiring you to find out."

"Uh-huh. You don't want to talk to him because, why? You think he'll run or . . . " The sentence trailed off.

"I slept with him last night."

Vidor said, "I'm glad I'm not your boyfriend."

"Go to hell."

"I'll be in touch," he replied. I set the phone down with a clang.

I was lying on the bed flipping through the pages of a mystery called *The Vines of Ferrara*. As I began the same paragraph for the fifth time, my attention wandered to the wall where, inexplicably, the shadows of the tree outside the window reminded me of Josh Mandel. That and everything else. What was this? Second adolescence? I picked up the book again and examined the cover.

There was a knock at the door. Expecting Larry, I hollered, "Come in."

Irene Gentry stepped in. I hopped off the bed, buttoning my shirt.

"Sit down, Henry," she said. She wore a suit in winter whites tailored to her body. It was quite a good body. "Do you mind if we visit for a while?"

"Of course not. Here," I said, bringing a chair up to the bed. "Sit down."

She arranged herself in the chair and extracted a silver cigarette case from her pocket. "May I?"

"Let me find you an ashtray." The best I could do was the soap dish from the bathroom. I held it out to her. She smiled and set it at the edge of the bed.

She puffed on her cigarette like a stevedore and said, finally, "I hate Sandy Blenheim."

"Any reason in particular?"

"It's so obvious that Tom's nothing to him but a meal ticket." She stubbed out her cigarette. "He pushes Tom to take whatever crap's offered to him. Anything to bring in money." She paused and looked at me. "I suppose you wonder what Tom is to me."

"It's not my business to wonder that."

She smiled without amusement. "I'll tell you anyway, Henry, since you're bound to hear rumors. I love him."

In the musty stillness of the room, the words were startlingly clear. Rennie studied my face and said, "You seem surprised."

"I'm sorry if I do."

"We all love according to our natures," she continued. "You, of all people, should understand that."

"I don't doubt you," I replied.

"Scoot over," she said, and kicked off her shoes. She climbed up on the bed beside me. "Larry says you're from San Francisco."

"Close enough," I replied, and explained that I actually lived in a small university town on the peninsula.

"Linden University? Did you go to school there?"

"Yes."

"That's wonderful," she replied, shifting her weight so that our bodies touched. "The closest I ever came to higher education was doing summer stock in Ann Arbor."

I put my arm around her. Today she smelled faintly of lilac.

"May I ask you something?" she said, tipping her face toward mine.

"Sure."

"Are you and Larry lovers?"

"No," I replied.

"Oh," she said perplexed. "I thought that's why you were here, to take care of him."

Since she had told me she knew Larry was sick, it didn't seem worth being evasive. "Larry's not the type to allow himself to be taken care of."

"You don't seem the type either," she said. "Frankly — and I don't mean this badly — that always surprises me in gay men. They often seem so needy."

"Larry and I are just the other extreme," I replied. "It's a kind of psychological machismo. Not really much better than being constantly in need, when you get right down to it."

"And then there's Sandy," she said, her shoulders stiffening. "He defies types. I wish I knew why Tom keeps him around." She relaxed and said, "Is it really true that you don't need anyone?"

Perhaps because I had been thinking of Josh, the question tugged at my guts.

She must have seen it in my face. "Have I touched a sore spot?" she asked gently.

"It's just that I met someone."

"Last night?"

I nodded.

She closed her hand around mine. "Then shouldn't you be happy?"

"I don't think it's going to work out."

"The unlikeliest matches do, you know," she murmured.

Someone shouted her name from downstairs.

"Time to go," she said, swinging her legs over the edge of the bed. "Will you come and have lunch with me day after tomorrow?"

"I'd love to," I replied.

She put her shoes on, stood up and staightened her skirt. "Good, make it around noon. Larry can tell you where I live." She leaned over and kissed my cheek. "He's a fool if he lets you go," she said.

"Larry?"

"You know who I mean. Goodbye, Henry."

"Goodbye, Rennie," I replied and listened as she made her way down the stairs. I got up and went to the window. The Zanes were getting into the black Mercedes, Tom in front and Rennie in back. Sandy Blenheim got into the driver's seat. Sandy Blenheim was Gldnboy? Only in Hollywood, I thought, and watched as the car pulled away.

A few minutes later, Larry came in.

"They're gone," he announced, pacing the room.

"I heard them leave. I thought you weren't taking new clients."

He sat down. "I'm not. That was just a little consulting."

"It looked like the IBM litigation to me."

He picked up the soap dish that Rennie had used as an ashtray and lifted an eyebrow. "You and Mrs. Zane have a nice chat?"

"I like her," I said, taking exception to his tone.

"That's allowed, I suppose."

"You don't?"

He stood up and paced to the doorway of the study. "In this business it doesn't pay to like anyone very much." He ran his hand across a dusty bureau.

"That's very cynical," I said.

He smiled at me, wiping his dusty fingers on his trousers. "Are you going to tell me where you spent the night?"

"With Josh Mandel," I said, amazed at how lightly I was able to speak his name.

"The waiter-witness?" Larry asked. "That's a surprise."

"To me, too," I replied, not wanting to pursue it.

"Doesn't the canon of ethics proscribe screwing witnesses? Except on the witness stand, I mean."

"There is no case," I snapped.

"Sorry," he said. He looked at me. "Was it that good, Henry?"

"Can we talk about something else?"

"Evidently, it was," he said as if to himself. "Forgive me, I'm just jealous."

"You needn't be," I replied. "I don't expect I'll be seeing him again."

He sat at the foot of the bed. "I'm sorry," he said firmly. "I'm being a bitch." He held out his hand to me. "Friends?"

I took his hand and smiled. "Friends."

"Let me take you to lunch."

"Okay."

He stood up and looked around. "I haven't been up here in a long time," he said. "Never did like this room. Come get me when you're ready."

Only after he left did I remember that his lover, Ned, had killed himself here.

— 17 —

It was one of those winter days in Los Angeles when the wind has swept away the smog and the air is clear and the light still and everything has the immediacy of a dream. I parked on a street called Overland in the Hollywood Hills. It was lined with white-skinned birch trees. Their nude branches shimmered against the sky. Tattered yellow leaves clogged the gutters and the air was scented with the rainy smell of eucalyptus. There were no cars on the street and the houses were barely visible behind walls and fences and sweeping lawns that had never been trod upon except by gardeners.

I pressed the intercom button on a white wall. A moment later Rennie asked, "Henry?"

"Yes, it's me."

"You're on time," she observed.

"A bad habit of mine."

There was a buzz and I pushed a wooden door and found myself in a courtyard paved with cobblestones and lined with pots that bore flowering plants and miniature fruit trees. I crossed to the house, where a door formed of planks opened. Rennie stood in the doorway. Her hair was pulled back from her head. She wore black pants and a loose silk blouse the color of the sky. Three strands of pearls hung around her neck.

"Come inside," she said, after kissing me lightly on the lips.

We entered a long rectangular room. The ceiling was crossed with beams of rough pine. The walls were blindingly white and the tiled floor the color of dried roses. The furniture was Mexican country antiques. Over the fireplace was one of

Diego Rivera's lily paintings. Above a long sofa was a tapestry that looked like a Miro. A big round crystal vase on a table held a dozen long-stemmed white roses and stalks of eucalyptus.

"Lunch is almost ready," she said. "How about a drink?"

"Mineral water," I replied.

She went to a bar and poured a glass of Perrier and a small sherry and brought them to the sofa where I was sitting. I took the Perrier from her. She settled in beside me.

"*Salud*," she said, and we touched glasses. "I'm glad you came."

"So am I," I said. In the silence she seemed distant. I tried to think of things to say and settled, finally, on admiring her house.

"Thank you," Rennie replied. "It's my weakness. I bought it ten years ago with the only money I ever made in Hollywood."

"From movies?"

She laughed. "Oh, no. Real estate investments. I never made a cent out of the movies."

Just then, a squat Mexican woman in a lime-green frock appeared at the archway that led into the dining room and said, "Señora, lunch is ready."

"Thank you, Fe," Rennie said, and turning to me added, "It's so gorgeous out, I thought we'd eat on the patio."

She led me through the dining room onto a patio built around a small pool. The pool was fed by a stream that trickled from a concrete wall set into a hillside garden. Near the pool was a table set for two.

"Your husband?" I asked.

"He's at an interview," she said nervously. "He may show up later."

We sat down and I looked at her. The light picked out the lines that fanned from beneath her eyes. She looked tired.

"Is everything all right?" I asked.

"I'm sorry, Henry," she replied. "It has nothing to do with you. There was a scene with Sandy this morning."

"About what?"

"What else, Tom's career." The maid brought out salads and set them before us, a mix of sweet and bitter greens. She lifted

·133·

her fork, then put it down again. "Tom is an actor who can't act," she said. "My solution is for him to learn. Sandy's solution is for him to make all the money he can before he's found out."

The maid reappeared and poured Rennie a glass of wine. I shook my head as she tipped the bottle toward my glass.

"What's Tom's solution?" I asked, cutting a piece of lettuce.

"It depends on who talked to him last," she replied, grimly.

"Who's been responsible for his success?"

"He has," she said, abandoning any pretense at eating. She produced her cigarette case and lit a cigarette. "Some people are just so beautiful that life seems to speak to us through them — they're vital, radiant. Tom is like that. It's more startling in men than women, I think, because we don't usually let ourselves think of men that way. But Shakespeare knew. Remember the sonnets? 'Shall I compare thee to a summer's day,' was written to another man."

"Golden boy?" I offered.

"Something like that." The maid removed our salad plates and replaced them with plates of spinach pasta in a cream sauce. "I'm a fool for beautiful men," she added. "No doubt there are psychological explanations."

"To appreciate beauty?"

"It's more than that," she replied, tilting her head back to reveal the pouched skin beneath her chin. "I always wanted to be beautiful."

I began to speak but she cut me off.

"Don't say it, Henry. I'm not fishing for a compliment." She crushed her cigarette in a heavy marble ashtray. "I'm forty-seven years old. I look into the mirror and see my mother. When a woman reaches that point, she loses whatever illusions she has about being beautiful."

"Is it so important?"

She finished her wine. "It's life and death," she replied, "if you're not. You, of course, are."

I couldn't think of a reply that didn't sound wildly immodest or incredibly smug. "Thank you."

"You're embarrassed," she said, smiling.

"It's not something I think about."

"I thought homosexuals did," she said.

"I suppose that depends on which homosexuals you know," I replied.

The maid made another pass at the table, pouring more wine, bringing us plates of veal and baby carrots.

I heard tires squeal and then a door in the house slammed shut. The maid appeared with a frantic look on her face.

"Señora—" she began.

Rennie looked at her and then at me. "Henry, Tom's—"

Suddenly Tom Zane appeared at the doorway, drinking from a bottle of champagne. His face was flushed beneath his tan and his golden hair was disheveled.

"It's the ambassador," he said, recognizing me. "And, of course, my lovely wife."

He swayed above the table. The maid brought him a chair.

"Sorry I missed lunch," he slurred. "How's about a little apres-lunch drinky." He attempted to pour champagne into Rennie's wine glass. She moved it away and the champagne sloshed onto the table. He blotted it with the sleeve of his coat.

"I think you better eat something," Rennie said mildly and told the maid to bring him a sandwich.

"It's all right. I ate breakfast." He had trouble getting his mouth around the last word. The maid brought him a ham sandwich. He wolfed it down and asked for another.

"How was the interview?" I asked.

"The reporter was a dyke," he said. "She spent the whole goddamn time giving the eye to some broad at the next table." He looked genuinely injured as he related this. Another sandwich was brought to him.

"Was Sandy there?" Rennie asked.

"Hell," he said, his mouth full. "He was after the busboy. This town's a regular Sodom . . . Sodom and. . ." He looked at me for help.

"Gomorrah," I said.

"That's right, gonorrhea. You ever had the clap, Ambassador?"

I shook my head.

"Smart man," he said. "Keep your peter in your pocket. But you're queer, huh?"

Rennie said, "Tom, stop that."

"It's okay," Zane said. "I'm a little queer myself." He held up his hand and measured an inch between his thumb and forefinger. "Maybe this much." He shone a beautiful smile on me. "Maybe more."

"I think all people are basically bisexual," Rennie said, irrelevantly.

"That right?" Zane asked. "You ever made it with a dyke, honey?"

"You know I haven't," she replied.

"What about you, Ambassador? You fuck girls, too?" He looked at me, smiling. "I bet you're not even a real queer. I bet it's just a line. Does it work?"

"All the time," I replied.

He lowered his voice to a stage whisper. "You try it with Rennie?"

Rennie said, sharply, "You're drunk, Tom, and you're embarrassing my guest. Stop it."

He attempted a smile that withered under her gaze. To me he said, "Sorry. Too much to drink." He rose, stumblingly, from the table. "I need some sleep. Excuse me." He looked at Rennie who was lighting a cigarette. "I'm just tired, honey."

"I know," she said. "It's all right."

His face relaxed into a grin and he made his way into the house.

Rennie looked at me and shrugged. "Tom drinks too much," she said.

"I see that."

"There's nothing I can do about it."

"Probably not."

We talked for a few more minutes but it seemed her attention was wandering toward the direction of the house. I got up and excused myself. She walked me to the door.

"I'm sorry about all this," she said. "Can I see you again?"

"Of course," I replied. "Any time."

She kissed me and I headed across the courtyard to the street.

I had just opened the door to my car when I heard my name being called. I looked back at Rennie's house. Tom Zane was hurrying toward me.

"Let's go somewhere," he said. His breath was eighty proof.

"What are you talking about?"

"Come on, let's just go."

Rennie had appeared at the gate.

"You need to sleep it off," I said.

"Yeah, but not here."

I looked back at Rennie. Her arms were folded across her chest. She lifted her hand and waved at me. I looked at Tom. It would probably be a favor to her to take him away.

"Where to?"

"My house. On the beach."

"Get in," I said.

He got in and scooted across the driver's seat to the passenger side.

"Where are we going?"

"Malibu," he said.

Rennie had gone back into the house. I started up the car, made a U-turn and headed down to Sunset. By the time I got there Tom was asleep.

— 18 —

When we reached the ocean, I woke him.

"Where do I go from here?"

He sat up and got his bearings. "Right on the Coast Highway. Wake me up again when we get to Malibu." He shut his eyes and went back to sleep.

The blue sea glittered in the deep light of the winter afternoon. A few surfers in black wetsuits paddled out into the water and rode the slow waves back in, like children who dared the sea by wading a few feet into the surf and running back.

We reached Malibu, a strip of fast food places, surf shops, and bars. I woke Tom. He directed me off the highway down a narrow two-lane road that cut between meadows where horses grazed in the shade of big oaks. Here the light had a nimbus of gold and poured like a stream through the silty air. Tom had me turn down a dirt driveway to a small stucco house hidden from the road by a row of overgrown Italian cypresses. He stretched and opened the door.

"What's this?" he asked, picking up a card from beneath his leg. I glanced at it. It was the card that Tony Good had given me with his phone number.

"An admirer," I said.

He inspected the card, tossed it aside and got out of the car. I followed him to the door of the house. He fumbled with some keys and then let us in.

The living and dining rooms were combined into a single space. There was a counter along one wall, revealing the kitchen. A corridor led off from the main room to bedrooms and bathrooms. The place smelled of old fires and the fireplace held the charred remains of the last logs burned in it. The concrete floor was covered by threadbare carpets. A few sticks of old furniture were scattered haphazardly through the room. On the whole, the house was dark, chilly and quiet.

Tom looked at me and grinned. "What do you think?"

"Not exactly what I expected."

"I like to be comfortable. Rennie's house is like a museum."

His nap had sobered him up. I said as much.

"Booze doesn't have a big effect on me," he said as if he believed it. "It's warmer outside."

We went into the kitchen. He opened the refrigerator and pulled out a half-full bottle of Chardonnay. He led me outside to a covered patio. Weightlifting equipment was lying here and there, as were pieces of driftwood, sea shells, empty bottles of wine and beer. A bike leaned against a wall next to a battered surfboard and a wetsuit. A jock strap hung from a nail above a pile of firewood. Tom sat down on a canvas chair and invited me to pull up a chair next to him.

"I should get back to L.A.," I said.

"You can stay for a little while."

I pulled up a chaise longue and sat. An orange cat appeared at the far end of the yard and watched us.

"That your cat?"

"Only when she's hungry." He took a swallow of wine and passed the bottle.

"I don't drink."

"Never?"

"I'm an alcoholic."

Tom grinned at the cat and said, "Isn't that the point?"

The cat loped across the yard and came to the edge of the patio. She yawned and began to groom herself with quick, fastidious flicks of her tongue. Tom leaned forward, pulled off his blue polo shirt, and then sank back into his chair. His skin was as tawny as the little cat's fur. Even at rest, his elegant muscles seemed to quiver. He was kin to the little calico licking her paws at the edge of the patio; a great golden cat. He rolled his head toward me, lazily, and sketched the faintest smile at the corners of his lips. I imagine Narcissus had watched that smile form on the surface of a lake.

"It's quiet here," I said, to say something. "You come here to think."

"Thinking's not what I do best. That's Sandy's job. All my brains are in my face."

"Rennie doesn't much like Sandy," I observed.

He smiled distantly. "Sandy's all right. He knows what I am."

"And what's that?"

"A hustler," he replied. "Like Gaveston. You don't need brains to be a whore. Just a little luck and good timing."

"Rennie must see something else in you."

His face seemed to darken. "She knows, too," he said, then added, mockingly, "but she forgives me." He picked up his wine bottle and drank some more. "Poor Rennie," he muttered. "She brought me out here to shove me in the face of every producer who ever told her that she didn't have the looks to be a star. I've got the looks," he said, more to the cat than to me.

"She thinks she can turn you into an actor."

He set the wine bottle between his legs. "Who the hell cares."

"You did the play."

"I knew a guy like Edward," he said, lifting the bottle and drinking. "Someone I met in the joint." He studied my face and grinned. "Don't look so surprised, you're a lawyer — don't you know an ex-con when you see one?"

"Not always."

He tossed the empty bottle at the cat. She scampered but it caught her broadside. With a shriek, she hopped into the underbrush.

"I knew this guy," he continued, "only he wasn't a king, more like a queen, understand? A real lady." He laughed. "She was pretty and proud, like Edward."

"Were you lovers?"

He lurched forward in his chair. "Hell, no. I was just a punk trying not to get raped in the showers." He looked at me. "That's another story. But this queen was married to this big white dude."

"What happened to her?"

"The niggers got her," he said. "Beat the shit out of her, raped her, just to get back at her old man. She walked around for days like she had a broken bottle up her ass. Her old man didn't want her anymore. He said she led the niggers on. She never complained, never said anything bad about anyone." He stroked his chest, fitfully. "She just bought some pills and went to sleep."

"Suicide?" I asked.

"Yeah," he said, looking at me. "Like that kid you were defending. What's his name, Pears."

"He wasn't successful," I replied.

"That's a shame," Tom said. "I'd kill myself before I went back to the joint."

"What were you in for?"

"Being young and dumb," he said. "I'm going to get some more wine." He stood up.

"I've got to get back into town," I said, also standing. "You want a ride?"

"What's your hurry?" he asked, moving toward me. "You don't think I brought you out here just to talk?"

He unbuttoned my shirt and laid his hand against my chest. I stepped away. His hand dropped to his side.

"Don't you want me?" he asked.

"I wouldn't much like myself afterwards."

"That doesn't matter."

"It does to me."

He looked at me and then yawned. "You don't know what you just turned down."

"I think I do," I replied and walked away.

□

I pulled out of the long, dusty driveway and Tom's house disappeared behind the screen of trees. I rolled down the windows and the air poured in, blowing the card with Good's number across the seat to the floor. At the traffic light, I picked up the card and examined the drunken scrawl. There wasn't much to choose between Tom Zane and Tony Good, I thought, remembering Good's come-on at the party.

·141·

"You're kinda cute, Henry. You got a lover?"

No, that's what Josh Mandel said over the telephone the night Jim tried to kill himself. I looked up at the light as it flashed from red to green. That seemed wrong. Even drunk, Josh would never have said something as obvious as that. I crossed the intersection and merged into the traffic on the Coast Highway. And then I remembered something. There had been three calls that night. I had answered two of them. The third caller hung up before I could reach the phone. A car horn blared behind me. I glanced at the speedometer and saw that I had slowed to twenty. But my mind was racing, and, suddenly, I understood.

□

I stopped at the first phone I could find, which was in a bar called "Land's End." The receptionist at the Yellowtail informed me that Josh had called in sick and would give me neither his prognosis nor his home phone number. According to information, his number was unlisted. The cheerful male voice that gave me this data was sympathetic but would also not give me his number. The next call I made was to Freeman Vidor.

"I tried to call you," Freeman said, after the preliminaries. "That Mandel kid has run off."

"What do you mean, run off?" I asked, pressing a hand against my ear to drown out the background whine of Tammy Wynette.

"Hey," Freeman said impatiently. "He's gone, man."

"You're sure?" A thin woman in a halter and blue jeans smiled at me suggestively from her bar stool. I looked away.

"He was going to meet me this morning to tell me about that key," Freeman said. "He didn't show. The restaurant said he called in sick."

"Yeah, I talked to them." The halter had moved herself back into my line of vision. She gave me the finger.

"I went over to his place and looked around."

"You broke in, you mean."

"Whatever," Freeman said.

I glanced at my watch. "I want you to meet me at his apartment in about a half-hour."

"You don't believe me," he said, with mock offense.

"There might be a clue to where he's gone."

Now, truly offended, Freeman said, "You think I wouldn't pick up on that?"

"It's not just what you see," I said. "It's what you know."

"If you think screwing the guy gives you better insight—" Freeman began.

"I'm sorry, Freeman. I want to look around for myself, okay?"

"It's your money," he said, unmollified. "Thirty minutes."

"Right."

On my way out, the halter stopped me. She was drunk. Even in the black and red bar light she looked bad. "You talking to your boyfriend, honey?" she sneered.

"That's about the size of it," I answered.

— 19 —

Driving back from Malibu I got caught in a traffic jam on Sunset just west of UCLA and arrived at Josh's apartment twenty minutes late. Freeman was leaning over the railing on the second floor landing tipping cigarette ash into a potted plant. When he saw me, he made a show of consulting his Rolex.

"Traffic," I explained, coming up the stairs.

The door to the apartment was open. "And here I thought you were just being fashionably late."

"Is anyone home?" I asked, indicating the door.

"Come in and see for yourself," he said, and led the way. As soon as we stepped in, he disappeared into the kitchen. A moment later he came back with a bottle of beer. "You go ahead," he said. "I'll take notes."

There was a cigarette butt in the ashtray on the coffee table. Not a Winston, Josh's brand, but a Merit — what Freeman smoked. Otherwise the living room looked just as it had two nights earlier. Freeman followed me into the bedroom. The bed had been hastily thrown together, a blue blanket slipping to the floor beneath a red comforter, but this looked to be its normal condition. I sat down and examined the contents of the night stand. They consisted of a paperback edition of *Siddhartha*, fourteen pennies, a pack of matches from the Yellowtail, and an empty water glass smudged with fingerprints, some of them, doubtless, mine.

Freeman picked up the book and said, "I never could get into this."

"You just weren't a hippie."

"Who?"

"Am I supposed to remember all their names?"

"Stop it, Josh. I know you're not like that."

"Doug," he said. "He lives in a split-level condo on King's Road and he has a hot tub on his deck. We sat in the hot tub and drank a bottle of wine and then he fucked me." He glared at me.

"Is that the terrible secret you wouldn't tell me the other night?"

"Don't talk down to me," he said, his fingers quivering. "And no, that's not the terrible secret. Does it really matter to you?"

This time I knew the right answer. "Yes," I said.

He put the cigarette out and all the hardness slipped from his face. "Three months ago I got this little rash at the base of my — penis," he said. "I panicked. I was sure it was AIDS, so I ran out and took the antibody test. The rash was just a rash — going too long without wearing shorts or something. But the test came back positive."

"You know that test isn't completely accurate," I said, to cover the sudden pounding in my ears. "And anyway it only means you've been exposed to the virus, not that you'll get AIDS." My heart slowed down. "Half the gay men in California test positive."

"Did you take the test?" Josh asked, glaring at me.

"Yes."

"Did you test positive?"

"No," I said, but added, "There are false negatives, too, Josh."

"Is that supposed to make me feel better?" he snapped.

"I guess not." I looked at him. "Look, Josh—"

"That's why I ran away," he interrupted, "because I didn't want to have to tell you. Because I didn't tell you." He paused. "Before we made love."

"We didn't do anything risky," I replied.

"No," he said scornfully, "it wasn't worth it."

"Jesus, Josh, did you want to infect me?"

He lowered his eyes. "I'm sorry, Henry. I don't know what I'm saying."

"Then be quiet and listen to me," I said.

He reached for his cigarettes.

"And don't light another one of those."

He dropped his hand. "Sorry," he said.

"I've been driving all over L.A. looking for you," I said, "and it wasn't because I thought you killed Brian. Not really." I ran my hand through my hair. "I'm thirty-six years old, Josh. You have no idea how old that sounds to me, especially when I wake up in the morning alone." I paused. This was going to be harder than I thought. "I just have these feelings for you..." And then I couldn't think of anything else to say.

He looked at me. "I love you, too."

I nodded. "Then come here." He rose from his chair and joined me on the couch.

He sniffed. A trickle of snot glistened under his nose. I gave him my handkerchief. He blew his nose gravely.

"I'm so scared," he whispered, and began to cry.

I pulled him close and held him until I could feel the heat of his body through his sweater. I thought of all the rational things I should say but heard myself tell him, "I won't let anything happen to you."

He pulled away and looked at me, lifting his sleeve and wiping his nose. His eyes searched mine, slowly. I didn't look away. We both knew that what I'd just said was, on one level, impossible and, therefore, untrue. And yet we both knew I meant it, which made it true on a different level, the one that mattered between us now.

He brought his face forward and we kissed.

Just then the door opened. I saw Mrs. Mandel out of the corner of my eye. Behind her came a man who I recognized from the picture at Josh's apartment as Mr. Mandel.

"Joshua," Mr. Mandel said, "what is this?"

We moved apart. Josh said, "Mom, Dad, you'd better sit down. There's something I have to tell you."

□

Over the next eight hours, Josh not only told his parents that he was gay but that we were lovers and about the result of the antibody test. Mr. Mandel ordered me out of the house, relented, and alternately screamed at and wept for his son. Mrs. Mandel seemed to have been rendered catatonic.

Then, after the hysterics came the hard talk. Josh's sisters were called, one in Sacramento and one in Denver, and consulted. They came out heavily pro-Josh. His father brought down the Bible and read to us the passage in Leviticus that condemns homosexuality. That led to a long, rambling discussion about biblical fundamentalism which ended, predictably, in a stalemate.

Mrs. Mandel mourned for her unborn grandchildren. Josh said that he planned to have children. This silenced her. Silenced me, too. We talked for a long time about Jim Pears and how having to hide being gay had probably led him to kill someone. We talked about AIDS. This was the hardest part for all of us.

I argued that AIDS wasn't divine retribution on gay people any more than Tay-Sachs disease was God's commentary on Jews. Mr. Mandel bristled at the analogy but his wife diffused the tension with a series of surprisingly well-informed questions about AIDS. It occurred to me then that she had known Josh was gay all along. Even so, they both remained worried and frightened. So was Josh. So was I.

In the middle of all this, Mr. Mandel ordered pizza and we had an involved argument over the relative merits of anchovies. He and I wanted them. Josh and Mrs. Mandel resisted. The three of them went through a bottle of wine while I guzzled Perrier.

And then it was three o'clock in the morning and Mr. Mandel was apologizing for being sixty-two and needing his sleep.

Knees creaking and head throbbing, I got up to leave. "I need my coat," I said to Josh who was sitting on it.

"Wait," he said, amazement in his eyes. "You're not going to drive all the way back to Silver Lake now, are you?"

A long complex silence ensued.

"It's not that far," I said.

"Come on, Henry. You're exhausted." Josh looked at his parents. "You can't let him go out at this hour. The roads are full of drunks."

"Joshua," his father began.

"Dad," he said in a whine he must have perfected as a child. "It's just a matter of common courtesy. Let him sleep on the couch down here. Mom?"

"Silver Lake is — far away," she said, tentatively, looking at her husband. Then, more confidently she added, "The sofa folds out and there's a bathroom down here."

"Well, I'm going to bed," Mr. Mandel said. "You want to stay Henry, stay."

"Thank you," I said to his back.

Mrs. Mandel opened a closet and pulled out some sheets and blankets. She put them on the couch.

"It folds out," she said.

"Thanks."

We looked at each other, then she looked at Josh. "Go to bed, Josh."

"In a minute, Mom," he said. "I'll just help Henry with the couch."

Defeated, she murmured her good-nights and slipped out of the room. We listened to her footsteps as she climbed the stairs.

"What a little brat you are," I said.

"It isn't over yet, you know," Josh said.

"I know. I know."

"It might go on forever."

"One day at a time," I said and nuzzled him. "I'm really tired."

"Do you mind us not sleeping together?"

"This is their house," I said. "Let's make it easy on them. They're probably upstairs awake as it is."

"How do you know that?" he asked, smiling.

"Years of legal training," I replied and kissed him. He kept his lips closed. "Josh, that's not how to kiss."

"My saliva," he said, biting his lower lip. "It might carry the virus."

"In negligible amounts, if at all," I replied. "Let's not let this thing run our lives."

We kissed again, properly.

"Go to bed, Josh, and let your parents get some sleep."

He pulled himself up from the floor and said, "You know what's really going to drive them crazy, is when it sinks in that you're not Jewish."

I smiled, then, remembering, asked, "Josh, the night Jim tried to kill himself and you called me, you didn't actually speak to me, did you?"

He shook his head. "No, I hung up before you answered. Why?"

"Because someone else called, too," I said, "and I now know who it was."

"Is it important?"

"Could be," I replied. "Good night, Josh."

"I love you," he said, and slipped quietly from the room. I watched the last embers spark and burn themselves out. When I finally arranged myself on the couch, my last conscious thought was not of Josh but of Jim Pears.

— 20 —

I heard someone rattling around in the next room and sat up on the couch. It was eight in the morning and I felt as close to hungover as I had in two years. I put on my trousers and shirt and followed the noise into the kitchen where I found Mr. Mandel pouring himself a cup of coffee. He seemed startled to find me still there.

"You want a cup?" he asked.

"Thank you." I studied him. Short and slender, he so resembled Josh that it was like looking forty years into the future.

"You want some cake?" Mr. Mandel asked, unwrapping a crumb cake.

"No thanks," I replied. It made my teeth ache just to look at it.

He caught my expression. "I have a sweet tooth," he said. "So does Joshua."

"He likes chocolate," I volunteered, remembering a box of chocolate cookies I'd seen at his apartment.

"Anything chocolate," Mr. Mandel agreed. "And marzipan. He likes that."

He brought two cups of coffee to the table and then went back to the counter for his piece of cake. We sat down. He blew over the top of his coffee before sipping it. I noticed the thin gold wedding band he wore. The kitchen was filled with light and papered in a light blue wallpaper with a pattern of daisies. Copper aspic molds decorated the walls. All the appliances — refrigerator, microwave, dishwasher, Cuisinart — were spotlessly clean and new-looking. We were sitting at a little pine table.

"Your house," I said, tentatively, "is very nice."

"Selma," he replied, referring to his wife, "puts a lot of work into it. She wallpapered this room by herself."

"It looks professional."

"You sure you're not hungry? There's cereal, eggs."

"No, I don't eat much."

He looked at me appraisingly. "You are on the thin side. So, you live up in San Francisco."

"Not exactly. I live in a little town down the bay. It's where Linden University is located."

"Yes, Linden University," he said, impressed. "You go to school there?"

"Law school."

"Good," he said, taking a bite of his cake. "I wish I could get Joshie interested in something like law school."

"He's still pretty young."

This was the wrong thing to say. Mr. Mandel glared at me and then pressed the bottom of his fork into the little crumbs of sugar that had fallen from the cake to the plate.

"Mr. Mandel," I began.

"Listen," he said wearily. "We talked enough last night. We'll talk again. For now, let's just enjoy our coffee."

"Sure."

We enjoyed our coffee for five tense minutes. At the end of that time Mrs. Mandel came in, wearing a padded floral bathrobe and black Chinese slippers. She said her good-mornings and offered me breakfast.

"He doesn't eat," her husband informed her.

"But you should," she said. "You're so thin."

Our discussion of my weight was cut short by Josh's appearance. He was wearing a ratty plaid bathrobe, the original belt of which had apparently been lost and was replaced by a soiled necktie. His hair was completely disheveled, his glasses sat halfway down his nose and he cleared his throat loudly. Ignoring us, he poured himself a cup of coffee. He cut a piece of crumb cake which he ate at the counter, and then announced, "I'm starving."

The rest of us, who had been watching him, transfixed, came back to life.

"Good morning, Josh," his father said acerbically.

"Good morning," he replied crankily.

"What do you want, Joshie?" his mother asked.

"Scrambled eggs," he said, "with cheese. And matzoh brei. And sausage."

"Sausage he wants with matzoh brei," Mr. Mandel said, smiling at me. I smiled back, feeling like a complete intruder.

Josh smiled at me, too. That smile packed a lot of meaning and it was lost on no one. "How did you sleep, Henry?"

"Fine," I replied.

"Not me," he said. "I missed you."

Mr. Mandel said, "You say this to hurt your mother."

"Shut up, Sam," Mrs. Mandel snapped. "Get me the eggs out of the refrigerator, Josh." She turned to me and said, in a quavering voice, "You eat, too, Henry. You're too thin."

Mr. Mandel rose noisily from the table and left the room. Somewhere in the house a door slammed shut. Mrs. Mandel looked at us and said, "He's — it's going to take time." Then she began to weep.

□

I called Tony Good, got his answering machine, and left a message that I wanted to see him. Josh came into the room and sat on the ottoman at the foot of my chair.

"Who was that?" he asked.

"Business," I replied, not wanting to have to explain Tony Good to Josh. There were enough Tonys in the world — Josh would encounter one of them eventually. "You're full of little surprises," I added.

"You mean about not sleeping well."

I nodded.

"They have to get used to the idea," he replied, but his eyes were uncertain.

"You're right." We looked at each other. "I have a confession to make "

"What?"

"I never told my parents."

He cocked his head and stared at me. "You didn't? Why not?"

"I guess the easy answer is that they died before I got around to it," I replied. "But the honest answer is — I was afraid."

He scooted forward on the ottoman so that our knees touched and said, "I can't believe you're afraid of anything."

"No? Well, I try to stay outraged and that keeps me from being afraid. But—" I put my hand on his leg, "—I don't think that's going to work with how I feel about you."

He put his hand on mine. "You're not afraid of me."

"Not of you," I replied, "for you. I can't stand the idea that anyone or anything might hurt you."

He smiled and seemed, suddenly, older, quite my equal. "Don't think of me as a job, Henry. You don't need a reason to love me."

□

Just as I got to the door of Larry's house, it opened and I found myself face-to-face with a young woman carrying a clipboard.

"Excuse me," she said, and stepped aside to let me pass. Larry was standing behind her with two mugs in his hand. "Goodbye, Larry," she told him. "I'll call you tomorrow."

"Thanks Cindy."

"Goodbye," she said to me in a pleasant tone.

"Goodbye," I answered, puzzled. When she left I asked Larry who she was.

"My travel agent," he said, heading into the kitchen. I followed him. "Where have you been?"

"Are you going somewhere?"

"My question gets priority," he replied, rinsing the mugs in the sink and setting them in the dish rack. In his Levis and black turtleneck he looked spectrally thin.

"It's sort of a long story."

"Tell me while I fix myself something to eat. Do you want anything?"

Mrs. Mandel's ponderous breakfast was sitting in my stomach. "No."

I told Larry about the previous night's proceedings while he constructed an omelet. He brought it to the table where I joined him. Before he ate, he swallowed a fistful of vitamins, washing them down with cranberry juice. He cut an edge of the egg and ate it, chewing slowly but without much apparent pleasure.

"Josh sounds like a very smart boy," he said when I related

Josh's parting comment to me.

"Don't say boy. It makes me feel like a child molester."

Larry smiled. "Twenty-two is several years past the age of consent," he replied. "And you should stop thinking of yourself as an old man."

"I suppose. Anyway, I'm relieved that Josh didn't have anything to do with Brian Fox's murder."

Larry set down his fork. "You're still thinking about that?"

"Do you remember the night Jim Pears tried to kill himself?" I asked.

"How could I forget," he replied, grimly.

"The phone rang three times. The first time it was a drunk who told me that Jim was innocent. The second time it was the jail. The third time the caller hung up before I could answer." I poured myself a cup of coffee from the pot on the table. "I thought that the first caller was Josh."

"Why?" Larry asked, finishing his meal.

"I'd talked to him earlier and it was clear he wasn't telling the truth about where he'd been when Brian was killed. I just thought, I don't know, that he was trying to relieve his guilty conscience, but—" I sipped the coffee, "—this guy flirted with me."

"Really?" Larry asked, amused.

"It was strange in the context. But I still thought it was Josh. Well, Josh did call that night, but he was the third caller, the one who hung up before I could answer the phone."

Larry's eyebrow arched above his eye. "Do you know who the first caller was?"

"I think it was Tony Good," I replied.

Larry looked at me closely and said, "Why?"

"Something he said at the Zanes' party as you were leaving with him. Some words he used were the same words the first caller used," I said, remembering that on both occasions Good had said, *You're kind of cute, Henry. You gotta lover?* "And the way he insisted that I take his number. What I don't understand, though, is why Tony Good would know anything about Brian Fox's murder."

Larry lit a cigarette. He squinted slightly as the smoke rose into his eyes and said, "It was Tony."

"How do you know that?"

"He called again that night," Larry replied, tapping an ash into his plate.

"Why didn't you tell me then?"

He shook his head. "I didn't know he'd called before," he said, "and I wouldn't have had any reason to think he'd be calling you."

"But he would call you?" I asked.

Larry nodded. "I've known Tony for a long time," he said, smiling without humor. "And in many capacities. A drunken call in the middle of the night is about par for the course."

"What did he tell you?"

"Nothing," Larry said. "I mean nothing about you or Jim Pears. We just talked." He looked at me guiltily.

"You're sure?"

"Believe me, Henry, I had no idea." He pushed his plate away. "I told him I was sick." He shrugged. "That's what we talked about." He paused. "He went on a crying jag, but I'm sure he didn't mean anything by it."

"You didn't answer my question about whether you're taking a trip."

He picked up his plate and took it to the sink. "As a matter of fact," he said, sticking his cigarette beneath the tap, "I'm going to Paris on Friday."

"Day after tomorrow?"

He nodded, his back still turned to me.

"Why?"

"To check myself in at an AIDS clinic," he replied, coming back to the table.

"Isn't this kind of precipitous?"

He rolled up one sleeve of his turtleneck and held his arm out. There was what appeared to be a purple welt on his forearm, but it wasn't a welt. It was a lesion. I stared at it.

"Kaposi?" I asked.

"That's right," he said. "The first one appeared two weeks ago."

He covered his arm and slumped into a chair.

— 21 —

The kitchen clock had rattled off a full minute before I spoke. "Why Paris?"

"Anonymity," Larry answered, resting his chin on his hands. "And for treatment, of course. It's one of the centers of AIDS research."

"Then why anonymity?"

He rubbed a patch of dry skin at the corner of his mouth. "That's just my way," he said. "I've always done things in secret."

"But you're out," I replied. "You've been out for five years."

He looked at me with a helpless expression. "Henry," he said, "you don't understand. This has nothing to do with being out. This is about dying."

"No," I said, "I don't understand. Everyone who loves you is here."

"In this room," he replied, and looked at me. "You're all there is. Ned is dead. My family..." he shrugged dismissively. "My dying would be grist for the gossip mill but no one would really care. I couldn't stand it, Henry. Not the curiosity-seekers." His lips tightened. "Not to be an object lesson. I want some privacy for this. Some dignity."

"By crawling back into the closet to die?"

He winced.

"I'm sorry," I said.

"It's okay. I didn't expect you to understand. You're young and healthy and in love."

I felt as if I'd been cursed.

"Don't go," I pleaded.

"I'm afraid I—" The phone rang. Larry reached around and picked up the receiver. A moment later he said, "It's for you."

I took it from him. He got up and lit another cigarette.

"Hello," I said.

"Hi, handsome." It was Tony Good, returning the message I'd left on his machine.

We made arrangements to meet that night at ten at a bar in West Hollywood. I got up from the table and put the phone back. Larry was in his study, going through a pile of papers. Watching him, it occurred to me that I hardly knew him at all. It was as if all these years I'd been seeing him in profile and now that he turned his face to me, it was the face of a stranger.

"I have a million things to do before I leave," he said. "Some of them I'm going to ask you to finish for me once I'm gone."

"Sure. Of course."

He sat down behind his desk. "Don't take all this so hard."

"We're friends," I replied.

He didn't answer but picked up a folder, flipped through its pages, and withdrew a sheaf of papers.

"This is a copy of my will," he said, handing me the papers. "You're my executor. Take it, Henry."

Numbly, I accepted.

□

Freeman Vidor stepped into the Gold Coast wearing a pair of hiphuggers, a pink chenille pullover and about a dozen gold chains. He sauntered toward me, stopping conversation with each step.

"Jesus," I said, when he reached me. "This is a gay bar, not the Twilight Zone."

Freeman looked around the bar. There were a lot of Levis and flannel shirts, slacks and sweaters, even the odd suit, but his was the only chenille sweater to be seen in the place.

"Back to R. & D.," he said. "Is Good here yet?"

"No, I doubt if he'll be here any sooner than eleven," I replied. "Ten o'clock was just a negotiating point."

"How about a drink?"

"Sure. Pink lady, okay?"

"Screw you," he said, and in his deepest voice ordered a boilermaker.

"I want to talk to Good alone for a while," I said, when the drink came. "Then you join us."

"What am I supposed to do in the meantime?"

I looked at him and said, "Mingle, honey."

Tony Good walked in the door at five minutes past eleven. I watched him stand unsteadily, just inside the doorway, and swing his head around. I raised my hand and he nodded. He made his way through the crowded room until he was beside me. He was even better looking than I remembered. Black hair, blue eyes. Model perfect features. Only his teeth spoiled the package. They were small, sharp, and yellow. He climbed up onto the bar stool next to mine and ordered a Long Island Iced Tea. The bartender started pouring the five different liquors that went into the drink.

"You're not drinking?" Tony asked, indicating the bottle of mineral water in front of me.

"No," I said. "You go ahead." I paid for his drink.

"Here's looking at you, kid," he said in a tired Bogart voice, and knocked off a good third of the drink in a single swallow. "So," he said, crumpling a cocktail napkin, "is this a date or what?"

"You wanted to see me, Tony."

He squinted at me for a second, then said, "You called me, remember?"

I looked away from him and poured some mineral water in my glass. "Not the first time," I replied.

He took a sip of his drink. "You're cute, Henry, but not cute enough to play games."

"The first time you called," I said. "Back in October. You told me that you knew who killed Brian Fox."

Tony had worked his way down to the bottom of his drink. The bartender, without asking, starting pouring him another.

"Who the hell is Brian Fox?" he asked.

"Now you're playing games," I said, looking at him. I flicked my head and Freeman came across the room until he stood behind Tony. Tony looked over his shoulder and got an eyeful of pink chenille.

"Jesus, what's this?" he asked.

"Don't ask me to show my badge," Freeman said in a low voice. "It's bad for business."

Tony looked at Freeman and then at me. I waited for him to call Freeman's bluff. Instead, he picked up his drink, gestured to the bartender and told me, "Pay the man."

I paid for the drink. "So who was it, Tony?"

He churned his drink with a swizzle stick and answered, "Sandy."

"I want details," I said.

"First we gotta make a deal," he said. "I tell you what I know but it stays here, between us. You nail him some other way." He looked defiantly at Freeman and me.

"Okay," I said. "Go ahead."

"It was back about a year ago. We were in rehearsals on *Edward*. I came out back for a smoke and saw this kid hanging around the parking lot."

"Fox?" I asked.

He took a swallow of his drink and nodded. "Yeah, but he didn't say his name. He was kind of cute, so I started talking to him. I asked him what he was doing there, thinking maybe he was a hustler. He goes, 'I'm waiting for Goldenboy.'"

"Goldenboy?" Freeman asked.

"That's what I said," Good continued. "He points to Sandy's Mercedes. He's got this license plate on it—"

"It spells out Goldenboy," I said.

"You've seen it," Good said. "He tells me he's got to talk to Goldenboy, so I go, 'Don't you know his name?' The kid says 'Yeah, it's Sanford Blasenheim.'"

"Is that Sandy's real name?" I asked.

"Does that sound like a stage name to you?" Tony asked, smiling snidely. "Anyway, I know this kid doesn't know Sandy 'cause no one calls him by his real name."

Freeman asked, "So how did Fox know it?"

Tony had finished the drink and signaled the bartender for a third. "This is thirsty business," he said to me.

"How did Fox know?" I asked.

"He gave me some bullshit story about breaking into DMV's computer and running the license plate," he said.

I looked at Freeman. "Is that possible?"

"The kid knew his computers," Freeman said, "but that sounds like too much trouble. All's he had to do was call DMV and say he was in a hit-and-run with Blenheim's car and ask them to run the plate."

"DMV's pretty generous with their information," I observed.

"They don't get paid enough to care," Freeman replied.

Tony, who had been listening, broke in, "But how did he know about the license plate? He wouldn't tell me that."

"The parking lot," I said, still speaking to Freeman. "When he followed Jim and Sandy out to the car, he saw the license plate." I turned back to Tony. "What else happened, Tony?"

"Nothing," he said. "I tried to make a date with the kid, but he says he wasn't gay. So I told him, then you don't want to know Sandy, 'cause you're just his type. After rehearsal I came back outside and the kid was in the front seat of Sandy's car with Sandy. Then they took off."

"Is that the last time you saw Fox?" I asked.

"I saw his picture in the paper," Good said, slowly, "the day after he was killed."

"Why didn't you go to the cops?" Freeman asked.

Tony looked at me. "You saw me in the play. What did you think?"

"You were good," I said.

"Damn right," he said, easing himself off the bar stool. "I'm a fucking good actor. All I need is a break." He picked up his drink, took a gulp, then put it down. "I started out in that play as one of the soldiers in the first scene. Big fucking role. Two lines, two minutes. And I had to fuck Sandy to get even that. That pig."

"But you ended up as Gaveston," I answered. "You fuck Sandy for that, too?"

He smiled, showing his jagged little teeth. "Yeah, you could

·162·

say that. I told him I knew about the kid. I told him what he could give me to keep my mouth shut."

I nodded. "Then why did you call me?"

He set the drink on the counter with the over-delicate movements of a drunk. "'Cause I wanted someone else to know," he said, "and put the pig in jail where he belongs." He looked at his watch. "This has been lots of laughs, Henry, but I've got a client waiting for me."

He started away.

Freeman and I followed a few minutes later and stood in front of the bar.

"Do you still have friends at L.A.P.D.?" I asked.

Freeman half-smiled and replied, "You told that guy you'd keep the cops out of it."

I thought of Jim Pears whom I had not believed when he told me he was innocent. "I lied," I said.

Freeman said, "There's still a lot to explain. Pears was in the room. He was the only one."

"I know," I replied. I shrugged. "Maybe nothing'll come of it, but if it helps Jim it's worth it."

"Nothing's going to help Jim," Freeman said. He shivered from the cold.

"Get ahold of your cop friend in the morning," I said. "We'll get together and visit Tony. By the way, where did you get that sweater?"

Freeman laughed. "My ex-wife."

□

It was after midnight when I got to Larry's. I pulled into the garage and sat for a moment in the darkness. It was perfectly still. I began to fit things together.

Brian Fox had not gone to the restaurant to see Jim, but to meet Blenheim. It was Fox who took the back door key from the bar. He used it to let Blenheim inside. Then what? I closed my eyes and reconstructed the layout of the restaurant in my head. They went downstairs. Blenheim killed Brian. But without a struggle? How? I listened to my breathing, and rolled down the window. That part I didn't know yet.

I had to get Jim down into the cellar, too. Could it be that he and Blenheim had killed Brian together? The garage creaked. A breeze swept through like a sigh. Or had Jim come down after it was done? Blenheim would have heard the steps from the kitchen floor overhead. Steps. I opened my eyes. There were footsteps in the garage. I pulled myself up in my seat and glanced into the rearview mirror. A dark figure merged into the shadows and was coming up beside me.

Slowly, I opened the glove compartment and got out the flashlight. I prepared to flash the light in the intruder's eyes and push the door open on him. Now. I swung the light around and clicked it on, reaching, at the same time for the door handle. Then I stopped as the figure backed up against Larry's car.

It was Rennie.

— 22 —

"Henry!"

I clicked off the light and got out of the car. "It's all right."

"I thought you had a gun," she said, recovering her breath.

"I'm a lawyer, not a cowboy," I replied. "I can hardly see you in here. Let's go outside."

I reached for her hand, found it, and led her back out where the streetlamp illuminated the quiet street. Although she wore an overcoat, she was still shivering. I put my arm around her.

"Where did you come from?" I asked.

"My car," she answered, pointing to a white Mercedes parked at the curb just past the house. "I've been waiting for you."

"Why didn't you wait inside?"

"I needed to see you alone," she said. "I didn't want Larry to know."

Her shivering subsided. In the bright white light her face was tired but seemed much younger, sharper. This is how she looks on stage, I thought.

"Come back to my car with me," she half-pleaded. I followed her to the Mercedes and got in. The car reeked of cigarettes. The dashboard clock read 12:30.

"Tom's in trouble," she said abruptly.

"Go on."

She stared out into the street. "I was at home, alone, when there was a call from someone — male, asking for Tom. He wouldn't tell me who he was. I hung up." She glanced at me. "I know it's rude but the strangest people somehow get our number, fans, salesmen, you name it."

She was getting off the point. "What happened next?" I prompted.

"He called again. He demanded to talk to Tom. I told him Tom wasn't in and he said—" Shallow lines appeared across her forehead. "—that if I was lying it wouldn't save Tom, and if I wasn't, he would find him."

"That's it?"

"Yes," she nodded.

"But you must be used to crank calls," I said. "Why did this one bring you to me?"

She fumbled with her cigarette case and extracted a cigarette. I rolled down the window when she lit it. "I know I'm not being clear," she said. She exhaled, jerkily, a stream of smoke. "Tom goes to bars. Homosexual bars. He meets men, has sex with them, and comes home. He doesn't do it often. It's a part of his life we don't discuss."

"But you know about it."

She dug into the pocket of her overcoat and came up with a handful of matchbooks. "It's these," she said.

I examined them. They were all from local gay bars.

"He leaves them for me to see," she said, softly.

Some of the matchbooks had names and phone numbers written in them. "That seems cruel," I commented.

"To an outsider," she said, stubbing her cigarette out. She smiled, faintly, ironically. "Tom is — he doesn't lie very well. He can't bring himself to talk about this with me, but he won't lie about it, either. These," she nodded toward the matchbooks, "are his way of letting me know."

"Why?" I asked. "Aren't you the one who told me that discretion is the better part of marriage?"

"I'm more his mother than his wife," she said as if giving the time. "He depends on me to look after him. And I have a mother's intuition about him — when his hurts are real, when they're not," she continued with a sort of mocking tenderness. "When there's danger."

"Lawyers have a kind of intuition, too," I said, "and my intuition tells me that there's something you're holding back."

She was silent for a moment, then said, "I lied about the call. It wasn't anonymous."

"Who was it?"

"Sandy," she replied.

"Why would he threaten Tom?"

She shook her head. "I honestly don't know. There's something going on between them. Sandy's been completely out of control. He and Tom had a big fight a couple of days ago and Tom finally threw him out of the house. Then this." She shuddered. "I'm afraid, Henry. He's crazy. Help me find Tom."

I put aside the questions I wanted to ask her about Tom and Sandy. They seemed irrelevant when I remembered that Sandy Blenheim was a killer.

"You think he's at one of these places?" I asked, holding up the matchbooks.

"I don't know where else to look," she replied.

□

Last call had been called five minutes earlier but no one was moving. I walked around the bar again, the last in Tom's matchbook collection. The other three had also been like this, dark and out of the way, far from the glittery strip of Santa Monica Boulevard known by the locals as Boys Town with its trendy bars and discos.

This bar, The Keep, was on a Hollywood side street that had disappeared from the maps around 1930. There wasn't much to the place: a bar lined with stools where customers could sit and watch their reflections blur in the mirror as the night wore on, a small dance floor bathed in blue light, a few tables lit by orange candles. Posters of beefy naked men covered the walls. Many of the patrons were middle-aged or older, and the level of shrieking was pretty high. Definitely a pre-Stonewall scene.

I leaned against the wall and looked around. Half a dozen of the bar stools were occupied. A handsome man's reflection smiled at me. I smiled back and continued inspecting the other customers. Tom Zane was not among them.

As I started out the door, I heard someone say, "Ambassador."

I stopped. "Zane," I replied.

The skinny bartender jerked his head toward me, his long earring dangling against his cheek.

"You say something?" he asked me.

I shook my head and walked back to where I had been standing. The man in the mirror was still smiling. He wore a plaid shirt beneath a black leather jacket. He had dark hair and a moustache. His eyes were brown.

Holding his eye in the mirror, I stepped forward until I stood directly behind him. His smile widened.

"Zane?"

"Ambassador," he replied, and swung around on the bar stool until he faced me.

"I didn't recognize you at all."

"Were you trying to?"

"As a matter of fact, I was. Rennie sent me to find you."

He frowned. "Rennie?"

"There was a call tonight, threatening you. She brought your matchbook collection to me and sent me looking for you."

"Goddammit," he breathed. "What's wrong with her?"

"She was worried, Tom. The caller was Sandy."

He narrowed his eyes. "What did she tell you about Sandy?"

"That you had a fight and kicked him out of your house."

"Let's get out of here," he said. He dropped a ten dollar bill on the bar and we went out to the street. It was drizzling. The bar was in a warehouse district and, as we headed down the street toward Cahuenga, a Doberman sprang out from a fenced-in lot and barked. A woman in the tatters of a coat hurried by, stopped, and screamed invectives at the dog. We reached Cahuenga and Tom's car, a red Fiat Spider with a plate that read "Drifter."

"Where are you parked?" Tom asked.

"Just down the street."

"I think you should forget any of this happened," he said,

reaching to the moustache and pulling it from his face. I watched, fascinated.

"What about the eyes?" I asked.

"Brown contact lenses. The hair's just a colored mousse. Washes right out," he smiled. "It's Hollywood, Henry."

"Seems like a lot of trouble just to have a drink at a place like that."

"Haven't you ever wanted to be invisible, Henry?" he asked, opening the car door.

I shook my head.

"No," he said. "I guess you wouldn't miss what you haven't lost. Me, I can't walk down the street without some girl throwing her tits in my face or some fag groping me. Don't get me wrong. It's not like I'm down on sex, but I like to choose the time and the place." He got into the car and smiled. "You heard what I said about forgetting about tonight."

"I heard," I said, "but Sandy's about to have some other problems."

"Don't tell me anything," he said, starting up his car. "I'm finished with Sandy."

I looked at him. "Then you know," I said.

He shook his head. "I don't know anything. See you around, Henry." He put the car in gear and skidded off down the wet black street toward Sunset and, I hoped, home. I stood there for a minute, as if on an empty stage, and then started back to my car.

□

It was two-thirty-five when I knocked at the door to Josh's apartment. There was some noise from within and then he opened the door, drawing his robe around him. His hair was a sleepy tumble and his eyes beneath his glasses were tired.

"Hi," he said as I stepped into the warm room. There was a lamp on over the sofa and an open book on the floor.

"I'm sorry I'm so late."

"That's okay," he said and kissed me. "I'm happy you're here. I was just reading."

I took off my coat and tossed it to the sofa. The day had begun in the Mandels' kitchen, included Larry's revelation that he had contracted Kaposi, took in Tony Good's allegation that Blenheim killed Brian Fox, and ended in a Hollywood bar where a man with brown eyes watched me in a mirror. Images drifted across my brain with a lot of darkness between them.

"I'm exhausted," I said, smiling at Josh who watched me with dark, serious eyes. "How are you? How did things go with your folks after I left?"

He smiled, wearily. "As soon as you left they started in on me."

"I'm sorry, Josh," I said, and held him.

"It's okay," he replied uncertainly.

I kissed his warm cheek, feeling the faint stubble there against my lips. "Do they think I corrupted you?"

"It's not fair. I was gay before I met you."

"You can't expect them to be fair."

"Don't defend them," he said, momentarily, annoyed. "Sorry, Henry. I'm just tired."

"Let's go to bed then."

He yawned in agreement and we went into the bedroom. He got into bed while I undressed and washed my face and mouth at the bathroom sink. I slipped into bed beside him and we reached for each other, pressing the lengths of our bodies, one against the other, everything touching, foot, groin, belly, chest. In my mind — my relentless mind — I pictured our embrace, my exhausted thinness against his young sumpture, like a Durer etching of the embrace of youth with middle age. Thirty-six: that's middle age, isn't it? Midway down the road of life?

"You're thinking again," Josh whispered into my ear. "I can tell because your whole body gets stiff except one part."

I relaxed.

□

This dream I entered unwillingly because I knew where it would take me. I was sitting at the bar of The Keep, as thirsty as I had ever been. The bartender with the dangling earring refused to serve me because he said that I had stopped drinking. I looked into the mirror behind the bar. A stage illuminated by three blue lights formed in it.

As I watched I saw Tom Zane, naked, doing the last scene from *Edward the Second*, but instead of the black actor, Sandy Blenheim played the part of Lightborn. Blenheim was hugely fat, flesh almost dripping from his body, and wore only a jock strap. The scene was so grotesque I began to laugh.

"You think I'm funny?" Blenheim shrieked. "Then watch."

Suddenly he was holding a poker, with a red hot tip. He began to insert it into the anus of the body lying on the pallet on the stage. It should have been Zane, but it wasn't. It was Jim Pears, comatose and unable to protect himself.

"Stop it," I shouted. "Stop it!"

"Isn't this funny, isn't this funny," Blenheim yelled back.

I turned away from the scene to another part of the mirror. There, instead of my own reflection, I saw Larry's cadaverous face.

"Why is this happening?" I demanded of the bartender.

He looked at me. Now he had Mr. Mandel's face and he said, "Because you're a queer. A queer. A queer."

The last thing I remembered was ordering myself to wake up.

I opened my eyes. Josh, wide-eyed, had lifted his face above mine.

"Henry," he said.

I expelled a gust of pent-up breath. "It's all right. Bad dream."

He held me. I smelled his smells, felt his skin beneath my fingers and his hair against my face. At that moment, he was the only real thing in the world.

— 23 —

I left Josh the next morning and returned to Larry's house. I found him sitting at his desk writing checks.

"Did you see Tony last night?" he asked in response to my greeting. In the watery morning light he looked haggard but formidably alive, not at all the cadaver I had dreamt of the night before.

"Yes," I said, sitting down across from him. "He says Sandy Blenheim killed Brian Fox."

"That's unbelievable," Larry said.

I recounted for Larry the story that Good had told me. When I finished he nodded but his face remained skeptical.

"It sounds plausible," he said, finally.

"A plausible lie?" I asked.

He shook his head. "No, that's not it. Tony only lies to his advantage. I can't see how this would help him." He looked thoughtful. "And it's true about Sandy's taste for young boys."

"But you're not convinced."

"I still think Jim did it," he said quietly.

I stared at him. "Didn't you bring me down here to prove Jim's innocence?"

He smiled wanly. "Not exactly," he replied. "I wanted you to get him acquitted." He picked up a crystal paperweight from his desk and ran his fingers across its surface. "Look, I know what's bothering me about this Sandy business. It's that everyone knows Sandy's gay. The fact that he was caught having sex with a kid would have been embarrassing but not especially damaging." He set the paperweight down. "Not in this town, anyway. And another thing, Henry, don't you think the way Brian Fox was killed showed incredible rage?"

Remembering the pictures I had seen of the body, I nodded.

"Would Sandy Blenheim have that much anger inside of him?" he asked.

"How well do you know him?" I countered.

Larry shrugged. "Not very," he conceded.

"Well, someone who knows him better told me that she thinks he's crazy."

Larry squinted at me. "Who?"

"Irene Gentry."

He was silent for a moment. "Maybe," he said. "She would know, if anyone does, what he's really like. He practically lives with Tom and her."

"You want to believe it was Jim," I said. "Why?"

He looked away from me and said, slowly, "Because I want to believe that he was capable of fighting back."

"But not that way, Larry. Not by killing someone."

"You have strictures about killing that I don't share," he replied.

This seemed odd coming from a dying man.

"And anyway," he rubbed his eyes, "I loved him and you didn't."

"Who? Jim?"

He nodded.

"You never met him."

"I know," he said and looked past me to the window with its still view of the lake. "It's ridiculous, isn't it? A sick man's fantasy. I dreamed of bringing him here to live with me. I thought we could heal each other. How absurd."

"No," I said. "It isn't."

As if he hadn't heard, he said, "Does God give us life to want such things? It seems cruel."

"To love someone?"

"To fall in love with a picture in the newspaper," he said, "and to lie in bed at night like a schoolboy, unable to sleep because of it. To ask you to put your reputation on the line in the hope that you could work a miracle."

"But you were right," I said, fiercely. "Jim didn't do it."

"You don't understand, Henry," Larry said. "I wanted him to have done it, and I wanted the world to understand why."

"Meanwhile someone's dead," I answered.

"And how many of us have died at the hands of people like Brian Fox?" he demanded.

I glanced at the bills on his desk, from the newspaper, the utility companies, his gardener. Across the top of each of them he had written, "Discontinue service." I remembered he had told me that he was willing to trade his life for Jim's. At the time it had merely seemed like impassioned rhetoric. Now I knew he had meant it.

"I'm sorry," I said. "I'd like to agree but it goes against everything inside of me."

Larry smiled. "It's all right," he said. "I know you, Henry. You believe in the law the way other people believe in God. Not me. I'm dying. I only believe in balancing the accounts."

I went into the kitchen to call Freeman Vidor. He wasn't at his office. A moment after I hung up, the phone rang. It was Freeman.

"I'm at Tony Good's apartment with the L.A.P.D.," he said. "You better get over here."

"What happened?"

"He's been murdered," Freeman said. "Someone took a knife and rammed it up his guts."

"Up his—" I began to say, then I understood. "My God."

□

Over Tony Good's bed was a framed poster that showed James Dean walking down a New York street in the rain. On the bed were sky-blue sheets soaked with blood.

"He bled to death," a small man in wire-rimmed glasses was telling me. I wasn't sure who he was, the medical examiner maybe. There was a faint chemical smell in the air. Tony had been using poppers. My stomach heaved.

"Someone stuck him," I said, to say something.

"A twelve-inch blade," the little man said, "inserted into the anus."

I turned and hurried from the room into the kitchen where

Freeman was sitting at the table with Phillip Cresly, the L.A.P.D. detective assigned to the case. Cresly glanced at me without much interest as I pulled up a chair.

"You satisfied?" Cresly asked. He was a tall man with light brown hair, eyes that had been chiseled from a glacier and a twitchy little mouth. I thought I had seen his face before and then I remembered the picture in Freeman's office of the three young cops. A long time ago Cresly had been one of them.

"The bed was soaked with blood," I replied. "How can you say he didn't struggle?"

"Position of the body," Cresly replied as if reading from a list. "Nothing disturbed in the bedroom. Neighbors didn't hear anything."

"You really think he took a knife up his rectum without fighting?"

The ice-cube eyes considered me. "Vidor says the guy told you he was going to meet a client after he left the bar."

It took a moment for me to understand what he was implying. "You think that this is something gay men do?" I asked, unable to keep the astonishment out of my voice.

"I used to work vice," he said. "I seen movies where guys took fists up their ass. Jesus, I mean, right up to the elbow." He made a sour face. "A little knife is nothing."

I glanced at Freeman. A warning formed on his face. I ignored it.

"A little knife is nothing," I repeated. "You learn that at the academy?"

"I'm paid to do my job, Rios," he said, the mouth twitching. "But I don't have to like it."

I stood up. "What about Blenheim?"

"He's gone," Cresly said.

"You looking for him?"

"We'll find him," he said, smugly. "You have anything else to tell me?"

Freeman stood up, quickly, and pulled at my arm. "Come on, Henry," he said. I let him lead me from the room

"That jerk," I sputtered as soon as we were outside in front of Good's apartment building.

Freeman lit a cigarette. "The man's set in his ways," he said, mildly, "but he's a good cop, Henry. He don't like open files."

Two young men came down the sidewalk carrying an immense Christmas tree. They passed us with shy, domestic smiles.

"No struggle," I said, more to myself than to Freeman.

"Look," Freeman said, "the guy was drunk when we saw him. And he was probably dusted, too."

"PCP?" I said. "How do you figure?"

"I smelled ether in the bedroom," he said. He blew smoke out of the side of his mouth. "They use it to cover the smell."

"I know," I replied. "But that wasn't ether. It was amyl nitrite."

"Poppers?" Freeman shook his head. "I don't think so."

"What does it matter," I said. "He was obviously on something, but I can't believe it was enough to knock him out."

We got to Freeman's battered Accord. The license plate read, PRIVT I.

"It had to be Blenheim," I said.

"Yeah, that's what I figure. How do you think he found out that Good talked to us?" He leaned against the car, dropped his cigarette and crushed it.

"Maybe Good told him," I said. "Maybe he was Good's client last night, only the appointment wasn't for sex but a little more blackmail."

"Kinda stupid," Freeman observed.

"I doubt that Tony Good ever got any prizes for brains," I replied.

"What a way to go," Freeman said.

"Yeah. I think I better go pay a call on the Zanes."

"You think Blenheim will be going after them next?"

I nodded. "I bet Tom Zane knows everything."

"Poppers," Freeman said softly, tossing his cigarette to the ground. "Is it true that they make sex better?"

I shrugged. "All I ever got from them was a headache."

Freeman snickered. "Figures," he said. "You ain't exactly one for the wild side, are you Henry?"

"Not exactly," I agreed.

□

The Zanes were at home. Rennie, in a gray silk robe, arranged herself in a chair near the fire. The maid brought her tea. Tom was having his morning pick-me-up, a tall Bloody Mary that he mixed himself. He brought his drink into the living room and sat in the chair beside his wife. The two of them, blond, handsome, could have been brother and sister. They watched me with still, blue eyes. A fire crackled in the fireplace, releasing the scent of pine into the air. A Christmas tree had appeared in the corner, near the Diego Rivera, with expensively wrapped gifts piled beneath it.

I told them about Tony Good and Sandy Blenheim's disappearance. They said nothing though Rennie blanched when I described the manner of Tony's death.

I looked at Tom. "You knew Sandy killed Brian Fox," I said.

"How do you figure?" he asked, a lazy smile curling the edges of his lips.

"You produced the play," I said. "Blenheim couldn't have given Tony the part of Gaveston unless he cleared it with you. Isn't that right?"

He took a swallow of his drink. "You're a smart man," he said.

"You knew," I repeated.

He set the drink down and said, "Yeah, I knew all about Sandy's troubles."

"Why didn't you turn him in?" I asked. "The man's a murderer."

Rennie set her tea down with a clatter. "Don't say anything, Tom," she said. "Not without a lawyer."

"Henry is a lawyer," Tom replied. To me he said, "So it's like talking to a priest. Right?"

"If you tell me you've committed a crime, then I'd advise you to turn yourself in, but I wouldn't do it on my own."

"See, Rennie," Tom said, smiling. "These lawyers got all the angles covered." Tom looked at me. "I told you I did time in the joint, well, I was there more than once. It was a bad scene. I would kill myself before I went back there again."

I remembered he had told me the same thing that afternoon at Malibu a few days earlier. "Go on," I said.

"They picked me up for burglary," he said. "I managed to make bail." He picked up his drink and drank from it. "I split."

"Where was this?"

"A little town in Oklahoma," he said. "Shitsville. I did some hard years there, Henry. That's not important. The important thing is, I jumped bail." He finished his drink. "Sandy knew."

"He blackmailed you," I said.

"Yeah, that's about the size of it," Zane said, rising. He walked over to the bar and poured himself vodka and lime. Rennie lit a cigarette.

"But you're on TV," I said. "Aren't you afraid of being recognized?"

"It was fifteen years ago," Tom said, walking to the window that faced the terrace. "Hell, I could walk down the streets of that town and my mama wouldn't know me." For the first time I heard a twang in his voice.

"How old were you?" I asked.

He turned from the window. "Twenty-two." He smiled, bitterly. "I already done two years by then at a state pen. Got raped every night for the first six weeks till I married me some protection — a guy with a forty-inch chest and biceps I could swing from. That's how I stayed alive."

I glanced over at Rennie. Her cigarette had burned down to the filter and a chunk of ash dropped to the floor. She stared at the wall, her face without expression.

"You could use some protection now," I said. "You're Sandy's last hope. He'll be back looking for you."

"We can't very well go to the police," Rennie said, suddenly. She dropped the remnant of her cigarette into an ashtray.

"I understand that," I said, "but—"

"But nothing," Tom said. "I'll take care of Sandy if he comes back. In the meantime, Henry, you just don't worry about us. We'll be all right."

He stepped behind the chair where Rennie sat and rested his hands on her shoulders.

I stood up to leave. "You weren't Tom Zane, then," I said.

"No. I used to be Charlie Fry," he replied. "Poor little Charlie. He never had a chance."

— 24 —

Josh's VW was parked in front of Larry's house. I found them at the kitchen table, talking quietly over the remains of lunch, and sat down.

"I guess you've met," I said.

Josh said, "I hope you don't mind that I came here."

"Not me. Larry?"

Larry smiled. "I'm glad I finally met you, Josh." He looked at me. "What happened this morning?"

I summarized what I had seen at Tony Good's apartment and gave them an edited version of my conversation with the Zanes. I concluded, saying, "Blenheim could be anywhere. They may never catch him."

"Well, I guess I was wrong," Larry said.

Josh looked puzzled.

"Larry didn't think it was Blenheim," I said.

"Who did you think it was?" Josh asked.

"Jim," Larry said.

"But you've been helping him," Josh said.

Larry smiled at him. "Have Henry explain it to you sometime, Josh." He looked at me and said, "I'm closing up the house tomorrow. Of course you can stay as long as you want, Henry, but I imagine you'll be wanting to stay with Josh, anyway."

"You're really going through with it, then?" I asked.

"Yes," Larry said.

Josh looked back and forth between us. "What's going on?"

"I'm going on a trip," Larry said brightly, "to Paris."

"Great," Josh said enthusiastically.

Larry looked at me, then stood up. "Excuse me." He picked up their plates and carried them to the sink.

"Is something wrong?" Josh asked.

Larry rinsed the plates, set them in the dishwasher and said, "I'm going to Paris for treatment, Josh. I have AIDS."

Then he left the room.

,osh stared at me. "Is that true?"

"Yes."

"You can't let him go." His voice was spooked.

"I can't stop him," I replied.

He started to speak but said nothing. I could tell he was thinking about himself, about us. Finally he asked, "Would you let me go?"

"It won't come to that," I said firmly.

"But if it did?" There was fear in his face.

"No." I put my arm around him.

"I'm sorry about Larry," he said.

"I know," I replied. We sat in silence for a minute. "Josh, after Larry leaves, I'm going home."

He nodded. "I'm going with you," he said.

□

The next morning we drove Larry to the airport. He gave me the number of the clinic in Paris where he would be staying and a list of errands he had been unable to finish. We walked him to the gate. I remembered that all this had begun at another airport, in San Francisco. As the crowd swirled around us, we stood and looked at each other, not knowing what there was left to say.

He turned to Josh and said, "Take care of him."

"I will," Josh replied. "Goodbye, Larry."

They embraced like old friends.

Then he looked at me and said, "And you take care of Josh."

I knew I would never see him again. "Goodbye. I love you."

We embraced. "I love you, too," he said, and his lips brushed against my cheek. "Goodbye."

When we got back to Josh's apartment, I called Freeman Vidor and told him that I would be leaving for San Francisco in a couple of days.

"I have one last job for, you, though," I added.

"What's that, Henry?"

"I want you to keep your eye on Tom Zane for a few days, make sure nothing happens to him."

"You think Blenheim will be looking for him?" Freeman asked.

"If he's anywhere close."

"He could be in Tahiti by now," Freeman replied. "That's what the cops think."

"But just in case he's not."

"Sure, Henry," he replied. "Give me a number where I can reach you up there."

I gave him both my office and home numbers. "Listen, Freeman," I said, "it's been good working with you."

I could almost see him smile. "I travel, too," he said. "Anywhere, anytime. You just call."

"I'll do that."

□

We left Los Angeles one week before Christmas, choosing to drive up the coast in Josh's vw. We had made no plans about how long he would stay with me; he simply arranged to be away from the restaurant for a couple of weeks. Although things were vague, I wasn't worried because it seemed to me that the decision to be together had already been made and the mechanics would work themselves out.

As we drove out of L.A., my sense of belonging with Josh grew keener. It was partly the departure itself because, unlike other cities, one leaves Los Angeles by increments, from the crowded central city, over the canyons, through thickets of suburbs, until the tracts of houses thin into the remotest outskirts and then there are hills and sky and the freeway narrows to a two-lane road lined by eucalyptus, and the L.A. radio stations fade in and out, and it becomes possible to hear birds and smell the sea.

We stopped at a roadside produce stand and bought apples and oranges. Back in the car we drank coffee from a thermos and were silent, my hand in his when I wasn't shifting gears. The sky was clear and cold and the sun cast a rich winter light. Josh whistled under his breath, fidgeted in his seat, read to me from the L.A. *Times*, yawned, peeled an orange, carefully dividing the sections between us, closed his eyes, napped. I glanced up in the rear-view mirror and saw that I was smiling. I felt his eyes on me, looked at him. His lips parted slightly, and his forehead was creased by shallow lines. I tightened my hand around his and returned my attention to the road.

"I used to play a driving game with Larry," I said, "back when we were traveling around the state speaking against the sodomy law."

"What's the game called?" he asked.

I rolled my head back and forth to relieve the tension. "We called it 'Classic or Kitsch.' You know what kitsch is?"

"Sure," Josh answered. "My aunt's rhinestone glasses."

"Perfect example," I said. We were coming into San Luis Obispo. The traffic was heavier and the sky was clouding over. "The way it's played is, one of us chooses a category, like movies, and gives the name of the movie and the other one says if it's classic or kitsch."

Josh stretched and yawned. "What if you don't agree?"

"Then you have to say why." I glanced at him. "That's really the point of the game, the disagreements. You can learn a lot about someone that way. For instance, Larry and I argued all the way from Sacramento to Turlock about whether *All About Eve* was a classic or kitsch."

Josh looked at me. "What's *All About Eve?*"

"Are you serious?" I asked, turning my head to him.

He nodded. "Is it a movie?"

"Twenty-two," I muttered under my breath, grinning. "I can see your gay education has been sadly neglected."

"You mean there's more to it than —"

"Don't, Josh, I'm driving."

He moved his hand. "No, really, the game sounds like fun."

"Why don't you find a radio station," I suggested as i began to drizzle.

He fiddled with the radio until he found one that was audible above the static. He had tuned in the tail-end of a news broadcast and moved to find another channel. Then the announcer said, ". . . in other news, accused killer James Pears died today in an L.A. area hospital."

"Turn it up," I said.

The announcer's unctuous voice filled the little car as he continued. "Pears, a nineteen-year-old, was accused of killing another teenager, Brian Fox, almost a year ago today. Fox reputedly threatened to expose Pears as a homosexual. Last October, Pears attempted suicide before he could be brought to trial and he had been in a coma since that time. He died today of natural causes. Closer to home. . ."

Josh clicked off the radio. I turned on the windshield wipers and tried to focus on the road, but all I saw was Jim's face and all I heard was his voice, telling me he was innocent.

Josh said, "I can't believe it."

"This will make his parents' lawsuit more valuable," I replied, bitterly.

"What lawsuit?"

I shook my head. "Nothing."

"It's my fault," Josh said, miserably.

I glanced over at him. "Don't be ridiculous, Josh." It came out harder than I'd intended. "If anyone's to blame, it's me."

"That's not true."

"This isn't getting us anywhere."

We drove on in an unhappy silence. Finally Josh asked, "Why are you mad at me, Henry?"

Without taking my eyes off the road I said, "I'm not mad at you."

"Don't bullshit me," he said tensely.

I looked at him. He was staring straight ahead.

"I'm not mad," I repeated, more gently. "It's just not always easy for me to talk about what I feel."

"Is that why you've never said you love me?" he asked, abruptly. His eyes left the road and he looked at me. His mouth was grim. "You never have, you know."

"Joshua. . ."

He cut me off. "Don't call me that," he said irritably. "That's what my dad calls me when I'm about to get a lecture."

The rain had stopped. In the dying light of late afternoon I could see a smear of rainbow above billboards advertising motels and restaurants.

"We're both feeling bad about Jim," I said. "Let's not take it out on each other."

There was a long silence from his side of the car. Finally, he said, "Okay."

A few minutes later I looked over at him again. He was asleep.

"Will you be patient with me?"

He didn't say anything for a long time but finally put his hand on mine.

□

The day before Christmas I was leaning against a post at Macy's in Union Square watching Josh try on leather jackets. He had already gone through half a rack of them and had long ago stopped asking my opinion since I thought he looked good in all of them. This one though — dark brown in buttery leather — nearly inspired me to unsolicited advice but then I heard my name. I looked around. The man approaching me was smiling in the faintly supercilious way he used to disguise his shyness.

"Grant," I said, embracing him.

Grant Hancock pulled me close, crushing his costly overcoat, smelling, as he always did, of bay rum.

We released each other. His yellow hair had darkened and there were folds beneath his eyes and deepening lines on either side of his mouth but, generally, time made him more elegant rather than simply older. It had been a long time since I had seen him last.

"This is the last place on earth I would look for Henry Rios," he said, "so, of course, I find you here."

"And, when did you start buying off the rack?"

A salesman rushed by and jostled me. Over the din, I heard the slow movements of Pachelbel's Canon in D, a piece of music I had first heard in Grant's apartment when we had been law students together.

"We just ducked in for the ladies' room, actually," he said, apparently not hearing the music. I caught the "we." Grant had married two years earlier and was, I had heard, the father of a baby son.

"How is Marcia?" I asked.

"She's fine. We're parents now," he added, with a smile that ended at his eyes.

"Yes, I heard. Congratulations. What's your son's name?"

"William," he replied.

"After your father?" I asked.

"Yes. I'm surprised you remembered his name."

"I remember."

We stood looking into each other's eyes. The occasion — former lovers meeting after a long time — seemed to demand that something significant be said. But there wasn't anything to say, really, except that I was glad to see him and hoped he was happy. So I said it.

Before he could answer I noticed that Josh was standing before the mirror watching us. He slipped off the jacket he was wearing, tossed it over the rack, and walked over to us.

"Hi," he said, to me, and then to Grant.

"Josh, this is an old friend of mine, Grant. Grant, Josh."

They shook hands, murmuring pleasantries.

Grant said, "Those are very nice jackets you were looking at."

"Yeah," Josh said, "but a little out of my price range." Wordlessly, he snifted his weight so that our bodies touched and slipped his arm around my waist. "So," he said with unmistakable hostility, "how do you know Henry?"

"We went to law school together," Grant said, barely able to keep the amusement out of his voice. "And how do you know Henry?"

Josh said, "He's my lover."

"Well, you're very lucky, Josh," he said smiling. "Excuse me, I'd better go collect my wife. Give me a call sometime, Henry. Nice meeting you, Josh."

After he'd gone, Josh said, "Was I a schmuck?"

"If that word means what I think it does, the answer's yes."

"I'm sorry," he said. "I was jealous."

I put my arm around his shoulders. "Come on, I'll buy you dinner."

Outside the store I told Josh that I had to make a phone call and went back in. When I returned ten minutes later I was jamming a sales receipt into my pocket but Josh, who was talking to the Goodwill Santa Claus, didn't notice.

Over coffee, Josh said, "I guess we should be getting back home."

The waiter returned with my change. I tucked it into my pocket and said, "We're not going home."

"What do you mean?"

"Trust me," I replied.

□

The immense wreath on the door of the inn on South Van Ness was composed of aromatic pine branches twisted and laced into a shaggy circle and bound by a red velvet ribbon. From outside we could see the big Christmas tree that dominated the drawing room. A bearded man on a ladder was hanging gold ornaments on the topmost branches while a woman strung ropes of popcorn and cranberries around the bottom of the tree. Another woman, gray-haired and aproned, opened the door to let us in.

"Merry Christmas," she said, smelling of cookies and lavender. "Are you Mr. Rios and Mr. Mandel?"

"Yes," I said, as we stepped inside to the companionable heat. "Is the room ready?"

"Just come in and sign the register," she replied.

"Come on, Josh," I said, taking his hand. We followed her to a little counter where I signed us in. She handed me a heavy brass key.

"Second floor," she said. "Room 209. Come down later for carols and eggnog."

"Thank you," I said.

On the stairs Josh stopped me and said, "What is this, Henry?"

"A Hanukkah gift," I replied.

"This is great," he murmured as I led him up the stairs.

Our room had a fireplace. I knelt down in front of it and started a fire. The only other light was cast from the Tiffany lamps and the discreet overhead light above the mammoth four-poster bed. Wings of eucalyptus branches fanned out beneath the mantle of the fireplace, dispersing their rainy fragrance into the room.

This was one Victorian whose rooms fulfilled the promise of its beautifully restored facade. Our walls were papered in deep green with marbled swirls of pink and blue, as if abstracted from a peacock's feathers. The period furniture was comfortably arranged around the oval of the room. High above us in the dusky region of the ceiling, embossed brass caught the glint of the fire and lamplight. Our window looked out upon downtown's brilliant spires and a distant prospect of the Golden Gate.

From the bathroom Josh said, "Henry, look at this bathtub."

I went in. The big porcelain tub was supported by clawed feet The faucet, set into the wall, was a golden lion's head.

"Let's try it out," I said, putting my hands on his shoulders as he knelt inspecting the lion.

He looked up, smiling a little lewdly, and nodded.

We lit the bathroom with candles ordered up from downstairs and stuck them in the sink, on the toilet, at the edges of the tub. Josh lay with his back against me, dividing the water with his fingers. I kissed his bare shoulder, lay my hands lightly on his groin and felt the jerky movements of his penis. From downstairs we heard singing.

"I guess we missed the carols," I said later.

"And the eggnog." He pressed more deeply against me. "Thank you, Henry."

"The water's getting cold," I observed.

"Do we have to get out?" he asked.

"There's still the bed," I said.

"You're right," he replied, and pulled the plug to let the water drain.

While he was still in the bathroom, I pulled the package from beneath the bed and put it on the comforter. He emerged from the bathroom, drying himself, pushed his glasses up his nose and, with a half-smile, inspected the brightly wrapped box.

"More?" he asked.

"One more," I replied, sitting in a wing chair, drawing my robe around me. "Open it."

He tore into the package. "That's why you went back into

the store," he said, holding up the leather jacket that I had most admired him in. "It's beautiful, but Henry, it cost so much."

"Indulge me."

He slipped the jacket on. The deep brown caught the fading firelight and shone against his skin. But I wasn't really looking at the coat.

"It looks great on you," I said. My voice sounded unfamiliar to me.

He took the jacket off and carefully laid it across a chair. "I have a present for you, too," he said.

"What?"

He got his wallet out of his pants pocket and extracted a package from it. "Merry Christmas," he said.

I took the package and laughed. It was a pack of condoms decorated with a picture of Santa Claus.

□

I was awakened by the phone. I groped for it, picked up the receiver and mumbled a groggy hello.

It was Freeman Vidor. I listened to him for a few minutes, and then sat up in bed. "Are you sure?"

"Yeah," he said, "I'm sure. You better come down."

Josh reached out and stroked my leg. "Henry, who is it?"

"Shh," I said. "Not today, Freeman. Give me until tomorrow. Have you told Cresly?"

"I don't know if he'd buy it," Freeman replied.

"We need the cops," I said, swinging my legs over the edge of the bed. "We'll need all the help we can get."

He spoke for another couple of minutes and then, wishing me a Merry Christmas, hung up.

Josh was wide awake. "What's wrong? Is it Larry?"

"No," I replied. "It's about Jim. We have to get back to L.A."

— 25 —

Although I could not see his face, I knew that the man coming out of the men's room at the Texaco station had different color eyes than when he had gone in. In the front seat, Freeman nudged Cresly who was pressing the side of his face against the window, eyes closed. Sitting in the back, I watched Tom Zane get into his Fiat. A moment later, the Fiat's headlights flashed on and he slipped into the traffic on Highland Boulevard, heading north. Freeman started his car and we got in behind Zane.

Freeman said something to Cresly that I missed.

Cresly replied, "Yeah, let's bust him for using the toilet without buying gas." He lit a thin brown cigarette and rolled down the window. "Ain't this like old times," he said to no one in particular.

"You and Freeman were partners?" I asked, as we squealed to a stop just below Sunset.

"That's right," he said, "and even then Vidor got these hunches and dragged my ass all over town. Right, Freeman?"

"Hey, you're here, aren't you," Freeman replied, as we accelerated forward.

"Maybe," he said, "depending on what happens. If nothing happens, I was never here. This isn't police business yet."

The night sky was a dull red and there wasn't a flicker of natural light to be found in the heavens. Though New Year's Eve was four nights away, it was warm and gritty. We turned east on Hollywood Boulevard, a couple of cars behind the Fiat which now turned onto a side street and into the parking lot for the

Chinese Theater. Freeman followed but went past the lot, pulled up to the curb and parked. A couple of minutes later, Zane emerged from the lot and walked back toward the boulevard.

"You're sure he'll be coming this way?" I asked.

Freeman said, "He did before."

He switched on the radio to a classical music station. Cresly tossed his cigarette out the window and whistled beneath his breath. The dark, palm-lined street was deserted. The city looked like a gigantic backlot for *Day of the Locusts*. All that was needed was for someone to say "Action."

Headlights appeared in the rear-view mirror as a car crossed Hollywood Boulevard. When it passed, I saw it was an Escort bearing the sticker of a car rental agency on its back window.

"That's him," Freeman said, cutting off the last movement of Brahms's Third Symphony.

Cresly, who had been whistling the melody, sat up. "What are you waiting for?"

"This ain't a parade, Phil," Freeman replied.

Cresly spat out the window and muttered, "Feets don't fail me now."

When the Escort crossed the first intersection, Freeman started after it. At Santa Monica Boulevard, we turned right. Santa Monica was brightly lit and there was heavy traffic on the sidewalks, young men and boys standing on either side of the street, at bus stops and in doorways, watching the passing traffic. The Escort took a left at La Brea. Freeman let a couple of cars pass before he followed.

Our next turn was left onto Willoughby, a big street about four blocks south of Santa Monica. There were houses on the south side of Willoughby, but on the north side were the gloomy backs of industrial buildings.

"What's in there?" I asked, pointing at them.

"Office buildings," Freeman said. "Warehouses. Lots of dark places and no one around. That's where Zane takes his pick-ups."

"We're in West Hollywood now," Cresly said.

"This is a crazy place," I replied. "One minute you're in L.A.

and then you cross the street and you're in West Hollywood, but if you jog north you're back in L.A."

"L.A. surrounds West Hollywood," Cresly said, "and it's the sheriffs' turf."

At Highland, the Escort turned left, back up toward Santa Monica Boulevard, and, at Santa Monica, took another left back toward La Brea.

"He's going in circles," Cresly said.

"He's cruising," Freeman replied. He pulled off Santa Monica at Orange, the last cross-street before La Brea, and parked.

"Why are we stopping?" I asked.

"No point in getting him suspicious," Freeman answered. "He'll go around again, to get a good look at what's available, then he'll make his move."

I looked out the window. Two boys in tank tops sat on the bottom step of the entrance to a bank. Their collective age didn't add up to mine. One of them looked back at me, then at Freeman and Cresly. He nudged the other kid. They talked, got up and started moving away.

I pointed them out to Cresly. "They must think we're cops," I said.

"Probably they just think we're trouble," he replied. "Shitty life they got."

"Yeah," I said. "If Zane's been out here beating people up, wouldn't word spread?"

Freeman glanced at me over his shoulder. "He uses a different car. And he knows how to disguise himself."

"Anyway," Cresly added, "these kids come in by the busload every day, it seems. There's always some poor fucker willing to take a chance."

"There he is," Freeman said. I looked out the window to the other side of the street. The Escort was coming to a stop at the corner across from us. A dark-haired boy in tight jeans and a black jacket paced in front of a recording studio. He wasn't wearing a shirt beneath the jacket and when the Escort stopped, he flexed his arms, exposing his torso. He was a nice-looking kid. His dark hair made me think of Josh.

The boy stuck his head into the window of the Escort. A

minute later, he straightened himself, opened the door and got in. Zane signaled a right turn onto Orange. When he completed it, Freeman turned his key in the ignition. The engine whined, sputtered and died.

"Jumping Jesus," Cresly said.

I looked across the street. The rear lights of the Escort were just visible as Zane signaled a left turn into the warehouse district. Freeman grunted and turned the key again. There was a low roar and then nothing. The third time he tried the key, all we heard was a click.

"You flooded the goddam thing," Cresly snapped. He swung his head around to me. "Come on, Rios, let's go." He opened the door. "You," he barked at Freeman, "try to get this coonmobile working."

"Fuck you," Freeman shouted as we got out of the car. When there was a lull in the traffic we ran across the boulevard to the corner where Zane had picked up the hustler. We ran down Orange.

"He turned right at the first street," I said. A yellow junk-yard dog sprang out of the shadows from behind a wire fence and chased us, barking and snarling. We reached the intersection and stopped. The street was empty.

We were surrounded by low, dark buildings, fenced-in yards filled with machines, trucks, and stacks of wooden pallets, deserted parking lots and narrow alleys. Scattered streetlamps drizzled yellow light into the darkness. As we stood there, the loudest noise I heard was Cresly's labored breathing. He was in pretty bad shape for a thin man.

"Let's split up," he sputtered, and started walking down the street we had come to. I started off in the opposite direction. I glanced at my watch. It was a little after midnight.

Ten minutes later I was walking through an alley, checking the dumpsters and piles of lumber for the kid's body. Out of the darkness beside me, I heard a car start up. I looked toward the direction of the noise and saw a covered garage, open at either end, running the length of a brick building. At the far end of the garage the headlights of a car flashed on and it rolled toward me. I threw myself against the wall into the shadows and watched the car roar into the alley, skid a turn and race out. It was the Escort. There was one person in it. Zane.

When the Escort turned out of the alley I ran down the garage to where the car had been parked and found another dark street. Hearing footsteps behind me, I turned, my hands clenched into fists. It was Cresly.

"You hear a car?" he called, running toward me.

"Yeah, it was parked here."

We stood on the spot and looked around. There was an ivy-covered wall in front of the photo processing lab across the street. The iron gate set into the wall was slightly ajar. I glanced over at Cresly. He was also staring at the gate.

"Over there," he said in a soft voice.

We crossed the street to the gate and pushed it open. Between the wall and the building behind it, there was a grassy courtyard centered around an elm tree. A body lay beneath the tree, a male body, clad only in a black coat. As we approached him, a strong chemical odor drifted toward us. I had smelled the same odor, though fainter, in Tony Good's bedroom. I'd been wrong. It wasn't amyl nitrite.

"Smell that," I said to Cresly.

"Yeah," he replied, sniffing the air. "Ether."

The boy lay on his stomach. Cresly extracted a pen light from his pocket and flashed it as we knelt down beside the kid. Blood and semen trickled from his anus down his thigh. Cresly pressed his thumb into the front of the boy's neck.

"He's alive," he said, "just knocked out. Let's turn him over."

We rolled him over and Cresly focused the light on the boy's face. Close up, he had a faint resemblance to Josh. His lips were bloody and a slight discoloration was beginning to show beneath his right eye. A shallow gash bisected his chest below his nipples. Cresly opened the boy's jacket and with unexpected delicacy pressed his fingers along the boy's sides.

"No broken bones," he grunted and stood up. "Shit, what a mess."

"We've got to get him to a hospital," I said, also standing.

Cresly switched off the pen light.

"Did you hear me?" I said.

"Yeah, I heard." Cresly looked around and walked away, returning with the boy's pants and shoes. He set them on the grass beside the boy. "Help me get his pants on him."

We struggled with the jeans until we got the boy dressed. Cresly unbuttoned the flannel shirt he was wearing, took it off, and told me to help him get the boy into it. When we finished, Cresly said, "If we go to a hospital I'll have to flash my badge around to get him admitted."

I looked at him, shivering in his undershirt. "So?"

"I want to know there's been a crime before I do that."

I stared at him, slack jawed. "Rape?" I suggested. "Battery? ADW?"

"The kid's a whore."

"Goddammit, are you telling me that this is just an occupational hazard?"

"I'm telling you," he said, "that I'm not about to accuse the star of a fucking cop show of anything until I talk to the kid."

"That's the craziest thing I've ever heard," I said.

"You don't have to like it," Cresly said. "That's the way it is."

"You want to just leave him here, then?" I demanded.

Cresly shook his head. "Your buddy lives around here, doesn't he?"

"Josh? Yeah "

"Let's take the kid there. I'll get a statement and then decide about a hospital "

"He needs a doctor now."

"Yeah, I'll take care of that." He dusted off the knees of his trousers. "You stay here. I'll go see if Vidor got that car started." He started out the gate. "Trust me," he said.

"Sure," I muttered.

□

The boy's name was Robert and he claimed to be twenty, but I would have staked my bar card that he was no more than seventeen. We got him into bed at Josh's apartment where he was examined by an unshaved and slightly inebriated coroner — the only medical type to whom Cresly had ready access — who pronounced him alive and, except for superficial wounds and bruises, in good shape.

Robert said that after Zane picked him up "we drove around and smoked some grass. Then he parked and started getting all lovey, you know. Deep-kiss, that shit. I didn't go for that 'cause I'm not a queer but he said it was his money, so . . ." He sipped some water. "Then he goes, there's a place around here where we can go. We went to that place where you found me. He tells me to take down my pants 'cause he wants to suck me off. But he wants them all the way off. I'm getting kinda nervous 'cause this guy's way too good-looking to be a trick. I'm thinking he's a cop or something so I tell him, let's just forget it, man. Then he punches me, real hard, and knocks me on my ass. Next thing I know he's sitting on top of me with this switchblade, big mother, too."

Robert's hands trembled as he lifted the water glass to his lips and then set the glass down again. "He goes, shut your fucking mouth or I'll kill you Sure, I go, just don't hurt me. Then he cuts me here," the boy touched the scar across his chest. "He says, take off your pants. I take them off, still lying there on the ground. Then he goes, turn over. The next thing I know he's fucking me, not using any lube or nothin', just sticking it in. Jesus, that hurt, but if I scream or something he stops and pushes the knife into my neck, so I just bite my lip." The boy bit his bruised lips, flinched, and then continued. "He's really hurting me. It's like he's just fucking me to hurt me, not to get off or anything. I guess he came or something 'cause he was lying there on top of me. Then he starts saying these crazy things like, I'm going to cut off your balls, and, I'm going to shove this knife up your ass. Shit like that. But it sounds like he's gonna do it, really. So I start crying." Robert stopped and looked at us. "He turned me over, still sitting on me and he's got the knife and I'm telling him, don't hurt me, don't hurt me."

I heard Josh's quick breathing beside me. "He reaches into his pockets and pulls out this smelly rag. Next thing, he shoves it on my face and it's all wet and cold and then . . ." He broke off and wiped his face with the back of his hand. "I woke up in your car."

The boy lay his head back into the pillows. "I'm real tired," he said. "Are you guys the cops?"

Cresly nodded. A few minutes later, Robert was asleep.

— 26 —

We were at the kitchen table. Cresly and Freeman were deep into a six-pack of Bud while I drank coffee. Josh sat with his back against the wall, quietly watching us. The little apartment was still except for the ticking of the clock above the stove and, from the bedroom, the faint, ragged noise of Robert's breathing.

Cresly said, "If the kid sticks to his story, we got an ADW." He rubbed his icy eyes. "You tell me how we turn that into Tony Good's murder."

"Zane killed Fox and Blenheim, too," I said, hearing the tiredness in my voice. "He killed them all."

Cresly lit a cigarette. "One thing at a time."

"I asked Freeman to keep an eye on Zane," I began, "because I thought that Blenheim might try something. That's when I still believed that it was Blenheim who killed Fox and Good. But then Freeman — you tell him."

Freeman covered a yawn. "I tracked him for a week," he said. "Three times he went out to pick up a hustler. I didn't think I had to go make sure he got what he paid for, so I just hung around Santa Monica waiting for him to finish." He sipped his beer. "Third night I noticed that he always came back by himself. I got curious, so I drove around looking for the kid he'd picked up that night. I found him. He was holding up a wall, spitting out pieces of his mouth. He split when he saw me. Can't say that I blame him." He smiled wanly at his bottle.

"Everybody needs a hobby," Cresly said in a flat voice. The cold eyes were thawing — from exhaustion, I thought.

"When Freeman told me," I said, picking up the story, "it got me to thinking about Zane and Blenheim. They both liked boys." I glanced at Cresly, who frowned. "But everyone knew about Blenheim," I said, echoing what Larry Ross had told me. "If it had been Blenheim who picked Jim Pears up, the fact that Fox saw them wouldn't have been that serious. Probably not serious enough to make Blenheim a target for blackmail, much less to give him a motive to murder. But Zane, if it had been Zane in the parking lot that night . . . "

"In Blenheim's car," Cresly said, and reached for another beer. "That what you're thinking?"

I nodded. "The rented cars, the disguises. It all fits. Zane took Blenheim's car that night to go cruising. He got lucky at dinner with Pears, and took him to the car. Then Fox found them, got the license plate and traced it to Blenheim."

"That's how Blenheim found out," Freeman said. "When the Fox kid came to the theater looking for Goldenboy. He musta known it wasn't Blenheim—"

"No confusing Sandy Blenheim and Tom Zane," I added, picking up the cup of cold coffee.

"Blenheim figured it was Zane," Freeman said. "Talked to Zane about it. Zane told him to arrange the meeting with Fox."

"Fox met him at the restaurant," I said. "Let him in through the back. They went down to the cellar. That smell tonight, ether, you said. In the transcript of Pear's prelim the waitress who found Jim with Fox's body said the room they were in smelled like someone had broken a bottle of booze. It was ether. Zane knocked Fox out, then killed him.

"Jim Pears, meanwhile," I continued, my exhaustion gone, "thought that Fox was there to see him."

"Why?" Cresly growled.

"That's another story," I replied. "Just listen to me. I've been in that cellar. You can hear footsteps when someone is walking in the kitchen overhead. Zane heard the footsteps, knew someone was coming. He hid himself. When Jim Pears came down, he knocked him out like he knocked out Fox and the kid tonight."

"With the ether," Cresly said, sounding interested in spite of himself.

"Right. Then he saw it was Pears," I said. "He dragged Pears into the room where he had killed Fox, smeared Pears with blood, put the knife in his hand, and let himself out through the back door." I paused, remembering another detail of Andrea Lew's testimony. She'd said she'd looked for Jim out back. That meant the door had been left unlocked — by Zane. In that detail was the whole story, if only I'd paid attention. "Jim came to and then the waitress found him," I continued. "Jim claimed he didn't remember anything. The reason was because there was nothing for him to remember. But that didn't occur to anyone, so we all wrote it off as traumatic amnesia."

From his silent corner, Josh whispered, "He *was* innocent."

We all turned to look at him. "That's right," I said. "Innocent but with no way of explaining why."

"So that's Pears," Cresly said. "What about Good and Blenheim?"

"Blenheim first," I said. "Blenheim knew everything. Irene Gentry — Zane's wife — told me that Blenheim was acting crazy toward Zane just before Good's murder. She was lying, mostly." I stopped and the implications of what Rennie knew sank in for the first time. I pushed it aside for now. There would be time to think it all out later, but there was no denying that it hurt. "But there was some truth in it — Blenheim was probably pushing Zane around, a kind of blackmail, to get Zane to do things that would line Blenheim's pockets."

Cresly squinted. "What, taking money from him?"

I shook my head. "No, working him. Milking Zane for all he was worth because Blenheim got his cut, and it was probably more than ten percent."

"So Blenheim had to go," Freeman said. "But first Zane set it up so that it looked like it was Blenheim who killed Fox and who killed Good."

"Zane and his wife," I corrected. "She came to me the night Good was killed, saying Zane was in terrible danger. I chased through Hollywood looking for Zane while he was taking care of

Blenheim and Good. I was part of the alibi."

Cresly smiled, nastily. "Zane's wife, huh? You bi, or what?"

I let it pass.

"Zane had the motive to kill," I said, "and when Freeman told me that he liked to beat up his pick-ups, well, then it seemed like he had the capacity, too."

Cresly belched, softly. "No way to prove any of this unless Zane or his wife start talking. They won't," he added with dead certainty. "Even if we bust him for what he did tonight. Why should he?"

By the look on Freeman's face, I could see that Cresly's questions had stumped him, too.

"Nope," Cresly continued, picking up his beer. "Old Zane'll hire someone like you, Rios, to cut a deal with the D.A. If he pleads to anything, he'll walk with probation. Or maybe just continue the case until our victim there," he jutted his chin in the direction of the bedroom, "disappears."

He drained his beer and set the bottle down with a thud.

☐

After Freeman and Cresly left, Josh and I made up the couch in the living room and got into it. We lay there in the dark. I thought of Jim Pears who said he was innocent, and was, and Irene Gentry who pretended to be, and wasn't. Depending on what she knew she was an accomplice to at least two of the murders.

Now I let myself think about Rennie. She had played me for a fool with consummate skill. It was a flawless performance. Her task had been formidable: the seduction of a gay man. Since sex, the most direct avenue, was closed to her, she had had to resort to other methods. But she was a brilliant actress, keenly observant of the emotional states of those around her and capable of seemingly profound empathy. She understood me immediately from our first meeting when she told me I had the face of a man who felt too much. A born do-gooder. A rescuer. All she had to do was play a lady in distress.

Her role jibed with what she and Zane had planned from the outset, to divert the suspicion to Blenheim. They must have worked it all out months earlier, when I first came to town to defend Jim Pears. When Blenheim approached me about buying the rights to Jim's story, what he really wanted was to find out how much Jim remembered and what I knew. The three of them had conspired together at first.

Then, later, Rennie and Zane saw their chance to get rid of Blenheim and close the book on the Fox murder once and for all. So Rennie made Blenheim out to be the bad guy. Fortunately for her I disliked Blenheim enough to be an easy convert. After that, it was just a matter of timing.

But now things had unraveled. Why? Rennie was fearless but Zane proved to be the weak link. Another fragment of remembered conversation passed through my head, the actress at the cocktail party who referred to the Zanes as the Macbeths. There was a crucial distinction, though. Lady Macbeth goaded on her husband out of her own ambition. Irene Gentry acted from love. The only time I had ever seen her break character was the day she told me she loved Zane. What a terrifying love that must be to lead her into such darkness.

"You're thinking," Josh said.

"I know. I can't sleep."

"Me neither," he replied. There was a pause. "Do you want to make love?"

I kissed his forehead. "I don't really feel like it."

"Okay," he said. "What are you thinking about?"

I couldn't think of a way to tell him about the darkness, not yet, anyway, so I said, "Tom Zane told me he skipped out on a court appearance fifteen years ago. There's a warrant for his arrest out somewhere. I'll have to tell Cresly about it."

There was a long silence and then Josh said, "Is that all you were thinking about?"

"No." I turned and faced him, trying to make his face out.

"It's about Jim, isn't it?" he asked. "You feel bad because you didn't believe him."

I held him close, not answering.

"I feel the same way," he whispered. "I feel terrible about him."

"Not your fault," I murmured. Then we were quiet again, each with his own thoughts. A long time later we slept.

□

Someone was tugging at my shoulder. I opened my eyes to Josh's worried face and a sunny room.

"Robert's gone," Josh said.

I pulled myself up and stared at him. "What?"

"I got up and went into the bedroom to get to the bathroom. He's gone."

"Shit." I swung my feet over the edge of our makeshift bed to the floor. I got up and walked into the bedroom. The bed was disheveled but empty. "What time did you come in here?"

"Just now. I mean, ten minutes ago," Josh said, coming up behind me. "He took some things, too."

I looked at Josh. "What?"

"All the money in my wallet. Some clothes." He paused and sucked in air. "The leather jacket you gave me."

"I'm sorry, Josh," I said.

Josh attempted a smile. "He left me his."

"Great." The boy's jacket, cheap vinyl, was tossed across a chair. "I'd better call Cresly. They might be able to find him."

"They won't," Josh said, softly.

I nodded and went to make my call.

□

Cresly and Freeman arrived just before noon. I put down the tuna sandwich I was eating and answered the door. Their faces were grim.

"No luck?" I asked, as they came into the kitchen.

Cresly's eyes were at their iciest. "I can't believe the kid just fucking walked out of here," he said.

"We were asleep," I said.

"Yeah," he replied, accusingly. "Asleep."

"Look, Cresly, if you'd put him in a hospital instead of bringing him here—" I began.

"Cut it out," Freeman snapped. "The kid's gone."

"What about the warrant?" I asked, having earlier told Cresly about Zane's flight from the robbery charge in Oklahoma.

He shook his head. "Oklahoma went on computer just a couple of years ago with warrants," he said. "For fifteen years back they have to do a hand search. Could take weeks, if they still got the records."

"So now what?" I asked.

Cresly and Freeman exchanged a look. I didn't like it.

Freeman cleared his throat. "The cops want to set up a decoy," he said. "Bust Zane in the act."

"Put someone out on Santa Monica?" I asked.

"Yeah," Freeman said.

"Those boys don't wear many clothes," I said. "You won't be able to wire them for sound. Especially if Zane likes to cuddle before he beats them up."

"That's what the cops figure," Freeman said. "Besides, they're not going to get those kids to cooperate."

Cresly, who had been ominously silent, added, "Yeah, look at the kid who was here last night."

"So use cops," I said.

"We plan to," Cresly said, "but you know how it is. Put a cop in jeans and a tank top, teach him how to mince and lisp and he still looks, walks, and smells like a cop."

I glared at him. "Do you think this stuff up in advance or does it just come to you?"

"He's got a point," Freeman said.

"What's going on here, Freeman?"

"Maybe you noticed how much that kid last night looked like Josh," he said.

"Oh, no," I replied, shaking my head. "Absolutely not."

Freeman said, "Look, Henry. I've watched Zane in action. Josh is exactly the type he goes for."

"The cops get paid for it."

"You want to get Zane or what?" Cresly said.

"Not that much."

"Maybe Josh should decide," Freeman said quietly. "Where is he?"

As if on cue, the front door opened and Josh walked in wearing the black jacket that Robert had left. He smiled, uneasily, and tossed the mail on the coffee table.

"What's up?" he asked.

□

"I'll do it," Josh said, simply, after Freeman and Cresly finished their pitch. We were sitting around the kitchen table again. The ashtray had filled with butts as the afternoon wore on.

"No," I said, quietly. "You won't."

"I want to help," Josh said, looking at me with his dark, serious eyes.

I shook my head in response. The others were silent.

"I owe it to Jim," Josh said.

"Getting yourself killed won't be doing him any favors," I replied.

Cresly said, "No one's gonna get killed here."

I turned on him. "We're dealing with a guy who's already killed three people."

Cresly lit a cigarette. The smoke curled upward into the frosty winter light. "We don't know that he killed anyone yet," he said. "Anyway, he don't kill his dates. And we'll be there."

"How?" I demanded. "You can't wire Josh."

"We'll wire the car Zane rents," Cresly said, exhaling a snaky stream of smoke. "As soon as they get out of the car, we'll be there."

"See, Henry," Josh said.

"Bullshit."

Freeman said to Cresly, "Let's go for a walk, Phil. Let them talk."

Cresly smirked, but got up from the table. "Yeah, you guys talk," he said, "but let me give you something else to think about, Rios. Something washed up on Venice Beach last night. It used to be Sandy Blenheim."

He stalked out of the room.

"We'll be back in a while," Freeman said, following him out.

"You can't do this, Josh," I said. "Cresly's using you. I don't trust him."

"How else are they going to catch Zane?"

"There are other ways," I insisted.

"Like how?" he asked, lighting a cigarette.

"The warrant."

He smiled, wanly. "Cresly says they might never find it."

"Cresly could tell me the sun was going to set tonight and I'd still want a second opinion."

"Why do you hate him?" Josh asked, flicking a bit of ash from the sleeve of his sweater. " 'Cause he's a homophobe? The world's full of them," he continued, and added, "I was one. I called Jim Pears a faggot, just like the other guys at the restaurant." He looked at me, his lips a tight line. "I owe him."

"Not that much, Josh."

"If they had asked you, you'd do it. Wouldn't you?"

I didn't have to say anything because we both knew the answer.

— 27 —

Two nights after New Year's, I was sitting in an unmarked police car on Santa Monica Boulevard with Cresly, Freeman, and an officer named Daniels. The strip of the Boulevard between Highland and La Brea, usually packed with hustlers, was almost empty, the result of an earlier sweep by the L.A.P.D. The only hustlers left were actually cops with one exception ... Josh. He stood at the same corner where Robert had stood, wearing tight jeans, a polo shirt and the black vinyl jacket that Robert had left behind. He ran a hand through his hair and shifted his weight from one foot to the other.

A flat male voice described Zane's progress from Hollywood Boulevard, where he had just rented a Chevette rigged for sound. We and three other cars in the area would be able to monitor what went on in the car within a four block radius. Now there was nothing to do but wait.

'He looks real good out there," Cresly said, referring to Josh.

The radio crackled. "Subject is approaching on Sycamore. You should have him in sight momentarily."

Daniels said, "There."

I looked to where he was pointing. The Chevette turned right and started, slowly, toward La Brea. Cresly fiddled with the monitoring device and the next thing we heard was a rock song.

"What's that?" Freeman asked.

I listened. "Talking Heads."

Freeman looked at me blankly. Zane made three passes on the boulevard between Highland and La Brea, coming in and out of the range of the radio. Each time he seemed to slow a little when he passed Josh. The fourth time he signaled a turn onto the side street where Josh stood, turned, and pulled up at the curb. I watched Josh walk over to the car, just as Robert had, and stick his head into the window.

Josh said, "Hi. How's it going?"

"Can't complain," Zane replied, his voice watery from drinking. "You waiting for someone?"

There was silence.

Zane spoke again. "You wanna go for a ride? I've got some grass here."

"Sure," Josh said. My stomach clenched. I looked up and watched as he climbed into Zane's car. We heard the engine start up and then the Chevette drifted lazily down the street.

A match was struck. We heard someone sucking in air and then, in a tight voice, Zane said, "Take it."

More sucking noises. Cresly said to Daniels, "Follow them."

We pulled a turn across four lanes of traffic and drove down the street where the Chevette had gone. The only noises we heard were of the joint being smoked. A moment later, we got the Chevette in sight. It pulled over to the curb. We passed it. I resisted the temptation to glance over at Josh.

"So," we heard Zane say, "what's your name?"

Josh said, "Josh. What's yours?"

"Charlie," Zane said. "What are you into, Josh?"

We turned up the first street and headed back to Santa Monica, then turned back, making a circle, toward the Chevette. Cresly instructed Daniels to park just before we got to the street where the Chevette was parked.

Josh was saying, "Whatever, you know. Anything you want."

Cresly glanced at me without expression.

There was a movement in the Chevette. Josh laughed. "That tickles," he said.

Zane said, "Does this tickle?"

There was squeaking, rapid breathing, silence, then a slow breath and a sigh.

Daniels asked, "What's going on in there?"

"They're making out," I said. Daniels stared at me.

"Gross," he muttered.

Zane said, "That was nice. How come I haven't seen you around before?"

"I just got into town," Josh replied.

"I know someplace around here we can go," Zane said. "I'll give you a hundred bucks if you let me—" A sudden wave of static drowned out the rest of his sentence.

"Okay," Josh said.

We heard the engine start up. Cresly told Daniels, "Go around again."

We edged up to the intersection of the street where the Chevette was parked. Just as we turned, and the Chevette started moving, a black-and-white appeared from still another street.

"What the fuck," Cresly said, and yanked the transmitter from the radio, trying to signal the black-and-white It passed beneath a streetlight as it slowly approached the Chevette. It wasn't L.A.P.D. but the county sheriffs who had, apparently, drifted across the county line into the city. A flashlight flared from within the black-and-white as it pulled up beside the Chevette.

Zane said, "Shit." He gunned the motor and made a run for Highland. The black-and-white's red lights flashed and we heard it order Zane to pull over.

We pulled out behind the sheriffs. Cresly was screaming into the radio trying to stop them from giving chase.

"Clear out!" Cresly was yelling. Abruptly, the black-and-white stopped. Over the radio, someone was asking for clarification. The Chevette, however, was gone.

We came up beside the sheriffs. Cresly rolled the window down and continued screaming at the driver. A couple of minutes later he slumped into the seat, breathing hard. He picked up the transmitter and canvassed the other L.A.P.D. cars in the area. Finally, he turned to me and said, "We lost them."

"What!"

"I said we lost them, goddammit. Put out an APB," he snapped at Daniels.

I listened as Daniels gave an urgent description of the Chevette and its passengers.

Cresly looked at me again. "Where would he go, Rios? Home?"

"Not likely 'f his wife is there," I replied, trying to keep my panic in check. "Maybe he'll just drop Josh off and call it a night. You might have someone watching the car rental place."

"That's covered," he said. "Anywhere else you can think of?"

"He has a place in Malibu," I said, finally.

"What's the address?"

"I don't know. His wife, she would know. I think I could get us in the neighborhood, though."

Cresly's mouth twitched. "All right," he said. "You tell us how to get there. I'll send a car to his wife and get the address to alert the sheriffs in Malibu. Can you think of anywhere else he might go?"

I shook my head.

Cresly ordered a car to go to Zane's house and get the Malibu address from Irene Gentry. Freeman, who had been stone silent, said, "I'm sorry, Henry."

"Let's hope you don't have anything to be sorry about."

"Where do we go?" Cresly asked.

"Out Sunset to the Coast Highway," I said, "then go north into Malibu."

"You heard the man," Cresly snapped at Daniels. He reached to the floor and came up with a siren which he stuck to the top of the car. We shot into the darkness, the siren whining and utter silence between us.

□

We sped through the city, its lights exploding around us like landmines. As we passed through UCLA, the radio crackled. I could not make out what was being said but a moment later, Cresly looked at me over his shoulder.

"We got an address from Zane's wife," he said. "Twenty-eight hundred Sweetwater Canyon Road. That sound right?"

"I never knew the address," I replied, "but I should be able to recognize the house."

Cresly relayed the address to the sheriffs in Malibu, who had already been alerted to what was happening.

"They'll probably beat us to him," Daniels, the other cop, said. He sounded disappointed.

I sat back in the seat. Freeman lit a cigarette. We passed a row of luxury condominium buildings lit up against the darkness of the January sky like ocean liners. A helicopter swept through the red skies. Traffic yielded in our wake and soon we were at the end of Sunset, facing the dark ocean at the end of the land. We turned onto the Coast Highway.

I considered the possibilities. If we found them at Malibu and Josh was unharmed, then there would be no reason to arrest Zane and no chance to link him to the murders he had committed. But if Josh was hurt — I stopped myself. If they were there at all. They could be anywhere in this catacomb of a city and anything could be happening. My body grew cold.

I looked out the window to the ocean. The last time I had been out here, the sea was alive with light. Now it swagged against the shore illuminated only by car headlights as they flickered, briefly, across the ocean's oily darkness. I thought of Sandy Blenheim, who had been disgorged by the sea only a few days earlier, and it was with relief that I turned away from the water as the highway twisted inland. Soon, the honky-tonk business district of Malibu sprang up around us. We passed the bar where I had stopped to call Freeman. The woman who had flipped me off might be there now, getting herself comfortably drunk.

Without warning, a seismic shiver worked its way up my spine. When it passed I found myself balling my hands into fists.

Freeman, sitting beside me, asked, "You okay?"

We skidded across an intersection. There was a Texaco station at the southwest corner and a road beside it that led off into darkness. Suddenly, I knew that that was the road that led to Zane's place.

"We're going the wrong way," I said.

Cresly said, "What?"

"The road where Zane lives. We just passed it."

"Sweetwater Canyon's up a ways," Daniels said tentatively.

"Don't you understand?" I said impatiently. "She lied to us."

"You sure?" Cresly asked, skeptically.

"I remember the gas station back there. That's where I turned."

There was silence in the front seat.

"We're wasting time," I snapped. "Cresly..."

Almost at that instant, the radio flared up. This time I could hear what was being said. Twenty-eight hundred Sweetwater Canyon Road was a vacant lot next to a trailer park.

"Turn around," Cresly said.

Daniels pulled a U-turn in a flurry of lights, squealing brakes and horns. Two minutes later we were back at the road by the gas station.

Cresly looked over his shoulder. "Where to?"

"It's not far," I said. "Kill the siren. You don't want him to panic."

"Right."

The dark trees swayed like ghosts along the road as the sea wind ripped through them. Out beyond the lights of Malibu, it was dark as a tomb. The landscape passed as if in a dream and yet I could feel we were coming to the place. The house behind the cypress. The ginger-colored cat. The charred wood in the fireplace. The trees came into view.

"There," I said. "There's a house behind those trees."

Daniels pulled into the driveway and we came to a lurching stop, just missing the white Mercedes that blocked the Chevette ahead of it.

"Someone beat us to him," Freeman said.

"That's his wife's car," I replied.

Our headlights caught a dark-coated figure at the door. It was Rennie.

"That's her," I said. Daniels killed the lights and we were in total darkness but for a faint orange light coming from behind the curtain of one of the windows at the front of the house. The curtain seemed to sway a bit as if the window were open.

As we got out of the car, Cresly said to Freeman, "You armed?"

Freeman grunted an assent.

To Daniels, he said, "Radio Malibu. Tell them where we are. Is there a back way out, Rios?"

"Yeah," I said, opening my door.

"Go around the back when you're finished, Daniels. Take your rover, but don't shine any lights. If he's armed, we don't want to give him a target." Cresly picked up his own rover — a handheld radio — and got out of the car. Our feet crunched the gravel as we made our way to the back of the Mercedes.

"What's she doing?" Cresly asked as we strained to see through the darkness. She made a movement. Cresly drew his gun.

"Mrs. Zane," he said, "I want you to move back here, move away from the door."

"Who are you?" she demanded.

"The police, Mrs. Zane."

He's listening to us, I thought, watching the fluttering of the curtain at the window. Zane was inside listening. Suddenly, the light went out and then there was an explosion. A bullet sizzled through the darkness, within inches of where I stood. I dropped to my knees.

Daniels, kneeling beside me, said, "Draw his fire, while I get around back."

"No," I said. "Josh might be in there. You'll endanger him. And her."

Cresly said, "Move around the cars, Daniels. Just go slow."

"Tom! Tom! Let me in!" Rennie pounded on the door, shattering the stillness. Daniels scurried around the cars and quickly eased himself over the fence at the side of the house. Rennie screamed to be let in.

From within the house, Zane shouted. "Get back, Rennie! It's all over. Just get away."

She seemed to collapse against the door. I started toward her.

"Rios, stop," Cresly said in a fierce whisper.

Ignoring him, I squatted and darted to the porch. She sat with her back against the door, her face barely discernible in the darkness but when I whispered, "Rennie," she looked up at me, her eyes glittering.

"It's Henry. Come on." I reached my hand for her and she slapped it away.

"They'll kill him," she sobbed.

I half-lifted, half-dragged her up to her feet. "There's no time for this," I said. "The cops are here and more are on their way. You'll get caught in the crossfire. Let's go."

She struggled for a moment longer. "He won't let me in," she cried, then she let me pull her back toward the cars. I sat her down on the ground. Freeman was there, his gun drawn, looking into the darkness.

"Where's Cresly?"

"Out there," he said, nodding at a shadowy flicker of movement between a couple of trees.

"What's he doing?"

"He's gonna draw Zane's fire while Daniels breaks in through the back."

"Josh is in there," I said.

Just then, we heard Cresly from the other side of the yard say, "Zane. If the boy's in there with you, let him come out."

He was answered with another shot.

"Is that his evidence?" I demanded. I started toward Cresly, but Freeman pulled me back.

"You can't go out there, man."

"We don't know whether Josh is in there or not."

"Then ask her," Freeman said, jutting his chin at Rennie.

I knelt beside her. Her hair was disheveled and a silvery line of snot ran from her nose to her upper lip. Her face was slack and she looked old. Older than I had ever seen her before.

"Is Tom in there alone?" I asked.

She looked at me without apparent recognition and swayed her head back and forth.

I grabbed her by the shoulders. "Listen to me. Who's in the house?"

She turned her head away from me, lay her cheek against the car and muttered, "What does it matter. They're going to kill him."

Cresly yelled out, "Let the boy go, Zane. If he's okay we don't have anything on you."

I dug my hands deeper into her shoulders and shook her. "Tell me!"

She drew a long, shaky breath. "Is what he said true?"

"Yes," I said. "They know about the murders but they don't have any hard evidence. Tonight was a set-up. The boy was bait. If he's all right, they can't charge Tom with anything."

Even as I spoke I heard sirens, far off, but approaching.

"I heard another voice," she said. "Male."

I released her shoulders and crawled over to Freeman. "She says she heard Josh in there. I've got to tell Cresly."

"I'll go," Freeman said. "Watch her."

The sirens were coming closer. "Hurry, before the sheriffs get here. They'll scare him into something stupid."

"Zane?" he asked, confused.

"Cresly. Go on."

Freeman jumped into the darkness and disappeared, with only the crackle of grass, leaves, and twigs to mark his path. I returned to Rennie. The sirens. If Zane couldn't hear them by now, he soon would. I thought of Daniels alone in the back of the house.

"Did you just lie to me, Henry?" Rennie asked, in a semblance of her old voice.

"I'm just trying to avoid any more killing," I said.

She wiped her nose on her sleeve and said, "What hate you must feel for me."

"The boy in there is my lover," I replied, "and right now I don't feel anything about anyone except for him."

"But how—" she began.

"There's no time to explain." From their sirens, I guessed the sheriffs had found the road. "But if anything happens to him, I'll—"

"You don't have to threaten me," she said. "I understand."

I nodded. Someone tugged at my elbow. I swung around and found Cresly beside me.

"What the hell's going on here?" he demanded.

"She says she heard Josh in there."

"Bullshit." He bit off the word. "If he was in there, or still alive, Zane woulda used him to buy his way out. I'm sending Daniels in."

"You can't," I said, but he was reaching for his radio.

Then, three things happened, separated by only a matter of seconds yet seeming to span an eternity. The sirens screamed in my ears. I looked around and saw the first sheriff's car flash through the trees. Then, I turned back to Cresly who had lifted his rover to his mouth and swung at him wildly, knocking the radio to the ground. He looked up at me, fury and amazement spreading across his face. As he reached for the radio, there was a shot from within the house. We swiveled around. Rennie screamed. There was another shot and then, as its echo faded, doors slammed, voices cried out and the yard was full of cops moving toward the house, guns drawn.

"Don't shoot," Cresly shouted. "I got a man in there."

The sheriffs stopped in their tracks. A deputy hurried over to us. "What is this?"

"Keep your men back," Cresly said and picked up his radio. "Daniels."

"I'm right here," Daniels answered. "Out back. Something's going on in there."

We all looked toward the house. The porch light flashed on. Cresly stood up and shouted, "This is your last chance before we start shooting. Come out with your hands on your head."

Slowly, the door opened. My breath caught in my throat as someone stepped out onto the porch, hands raised high over his head. It was Josh. I breathed.

□

We were sitting on the porch steps. I had wrapped my coat around Josh's shoulders and put my arm around him, but he could not stop shivering or talking, even as he cried. He simply talked through his tears.

"It happened so fast," he said. "He had me sitting by the fireplace with the gun on me. Then we heard the sirens and he looked out the window. Just for a second. I grabbed the poker and just swung. It was dark and I couldn't see very well but I must have hit his hand because the gun went off and then I

·214·

heard it hit the floor. I went for it and when I got it I just started shooting — I just..." He broke off, sobbing.

I held him closer. "It's all right, Josh."

"But I killed him, Henry."

"He had the poker," I said.

"But I couldn't see that," Josh said. "I didn't wait to see what would happen."

"Thank God for that," I said. He buried his face in my chest. I looked above his head into the room behind us. A sheriff knelt beside Zane's body. Someone laughed. Someone sipped from a cup of coffee.

Irene Gentry stood with her back against the wall. Cresly walked up to her and said something. She shook her head slowly, again and again, until he shrugged and walked away. After he'd gone, she lifted a slender hand and, almost contemptuously, wiped the tears from her face. As if aware she was being watched, she looked slowly around the room and then out the door until our eyes met. I tried to read their expression but she was far away. I heard her ask for a cigarette and she passed out of my view.

Josh asked, "What will happen to her?"

"If they can prove the murders, she could be indicted as an accomplice. If not," I shrugged. "I doubt that anything worse can happen to her than happened tonight."

He was quiet in my arms. Nothing worse could happen to her. She told me once that we each loved according to our natures and her nature had brought her to an empty place, where it was as easy to die as to love. I looked down at Josh. The light shone off his face. His eyes were full of questions to which I had no answer but one. But that one I could finally give.

"I love you, Josh," I said.